To Chris, Kaley, and Jake—the best miracles!

Published by B&H Publishing Group
Nashville, Tennessee

Dewey Decimal Classification: TO COME
Subject Heading: TO COME

Cover illustration by Alexandra Bye.

1 2 3 4 5 6 7 • 26 25 24 23 22

CONTENTS

Mae's bicycle tires kicked up orange dust while red lights flashed in the driveway behind her. Usually kids ran toward ambulance sirens, not away from them. But Mae wasn't curious. She knew why the ambulance was there.

Never mind it was her birthday.

She'd been in the backyard with her sister, parents, and her best friend, Jimmy Mac, admiring her birthday cake. It sat in the center of the picnic table. She'd taken a breath big enough to blow out all eleven candles when her sister began gasping for air. It was the second time this month. Shelby struggling to breathe.

Mae's older sister had been in a wheelchair since the time she'd outgrown a stroller. She had never walked or talked on account of when she was in her mama's stomach. The umbilical cord got tangled around her neck. It stayed tight for too long and cut off the oxygen to her brain. Shelby had something called cerebral palsy—the most severe type.

So instead of "Happy Birthday to You," it was the blaring noise of James and Ricky's ambulance. Mae was on a first-name basis with the town's paramedics partly because Jessup, Georgia, was a small town—population: 2,483, give or take. And partly because the paramedics showed up at her house on a semi-regular basis. Most of the time the scare—episode, seizure, whatever it was—wouldn't last long. But it didn't matter. It always caused a jumble of feelings for Mae. Fear. Helplessness. Guilt.

"Mae! Wait!" Jimmy Mac hollered. She turned and saw him standing in the middle of the street. He was wasting his breath. This was one of those times she'd rather be alone.

When Mae reached the four-way stop, she looked to the left. That way led to the river lined with rocks big enough for sitting on. It's where she usually went when things got scary for Shelby. When Mae wanted to get away and think, or, as her daddy said, escape.

Like the time, almost exactly two years ago—the day after Mae's ninth birthday—when Shelby had nearly died. And it was all Mae's fault.

Now here she was again. Instead of celebrating her eleventh birthday, Mae was feeling smaller than a gnat. But there was something different this time. Something pulling her in the opposite direction. A tiny voice whispering, *This way, Mae.*

She was one for listening to the little voice inside because when she ignored it, things tended to turn messy. Mostly because of her big mouth.

Like when she was in second grade and Dr. Heery had made her wear an eye patch on account of her lazy eye. It'd made no sense to her. "Why are you covering the good one?" she'd asked him. He explained the good eye had to be covered so the muscles in the lazy eye would get exercised.

At school, Bubba Duncan took to calling her "Patch," and Mae's inner voice told her to be the bigger second grader and ignore him. But during a game of dodgeball, it was "Patch this" and "Patch that"—and she couldn't help herself.

"At least my patch is gonna come off in three months. You'll always be double-wide, Double Wide," she'd hollered, launching the red ball toward him like a torpedo. Bubba was the size of an eighth grader in second grade.

The teacher on recess duty had only heard the double-wide part and saw the big red welt on Bubba's cheek. Mae got sentenced to a week of no recess and an apology letter. She got two more days after she wrote:

> Dear Bubba,
> I am sorry you are as big as a double-wide
>   trailer.
> ~~Yours truly,~~
> Mae Moore

Today, as Mae straddled her bike at the stop sign, the voice she heard was soft but sure. So instead of taking off for the river, she turned right.

Mae rode along the two-lane road for a quarter mile until Mrs. Willene Hampton pulled even with her. Her blue Buick was as big as a tank, and she had to holler over its clackety clanking. "Mae Ellen, how's your sister doing?"

"She's good—hasn't had an episode in over a month now." Mae stared straight ahead. She was a terrible liar, and her huge hazel eyes always gave her away.

"Glad to hear it. She's in my prayers," Mrs. Willene added.

"Mm-hmm," Mae hummed, hoping today's ambulance visit was a false alarm and Shelby would be just fine when she got back home.

"You be careful riding on the road. They'll give anybody a driver's license these days," Mrs. Willene said, waving as she drove off.

The Buick picked up speed and zigzagged across the centerline until it vanished down the hill.

She thought back to the day Mrs. Willene had gotten her car. Mae had been sitting on the bench outside the Piggly Wiggly where her mama worked as head cashier. She was eating a chocolate-chocolate chip cookie when Mrs. Willene drove down Main Street honking her horn. She pulled into the parking space reserved for the Employee of the Month, landing her front tire on the curb. Customers spilled out of the Piggly Wiggly and Smith's Hardware next door to see what the commotion was.

"Davis signed with the Braves! He went in the 35th round!" Mrs. Willene had shouted loud enough for the entire town to hear. "He went down to Cecil's this morning and bought me this here Buick with his signing money!"

But that was at least two years ago. Davis never made it past the single A team. Something about an out-of-control temper, back problems, and drugs. The Braves released him, and Jessup's high school hero had returned a nobody. And the car he bought from Cecil's Classic Used Cars turned out to be more lemon than classic.

Mae shook the cobwebs of that April loose. She needed to pick up speed if she was going to top the hill. She stood from her bicycle seat and pedaled hard. She'd gone this way before, but it didn't seem so steep in a car.

She finally reached the peak and stopped. Mae considered putting both feet on the handlebars and coasting all the way down or riding hands-free, arms straight in the air like she'd seen in the commercials for roller-coaster parks, when she noticed a sign on the side of the road:

HOPEWELL COMMUNITY CHURCH

DRIVE-THRU PRAYER

EVERY TUESDAY AND THURSDAY
3:30–6:00 P.M., ALL SUMMER

ALL WELCOME!

Drive-thru prayer? Mae wondered. Jessup had a drive-in movie theater where movies played after they'd shown in the sit-in theater, two towns over. Mae wondered if drive-thru prayer worked by hooking up the speaker to your car. Maybe folks at Hopewell thought it was a direct line to God.

What if? Mae thought as she lingered a second longer. *Nah.*

She hushed the tiny voice whispering inside her head. She remembered a few years back when she'd prayed for Shelby every single day. Mae was eight; Shelby eleven. But it hadn't mattered. Shelby still couldn't walk or talk or do what other sisters did. Mae decided then that praying didn't work. There wasn't any use in hoping things could be different.

She turned her bike around and headed for the river, remembering it was best to get used to things the way they were. Still, whenever Shelby had a seizure or trouble breathing, Mae couldn't get used to the look of fear on her parents' faces or the hurt in her own heart.

If only she could find a reason to hope again.

CHAPTER TWO

The next day, Mae and Jimmy Mac met on the baseball field behind the school. It was half dirt and half weeds but had a decent backstop.

Mae set her bat on the ground then threw the baseball high in the air, catching it in her glove. "Wanna catch pop flies?"

"No." Jimmy Mac tapped the basketball in his arms.

"Practice laying down bunts?" Mae punched her glove hard with the baseball.

"Not really." Jimmy Mac bounced his basketball on the ground. It landed on a rock and skittered away.

Mae stopped it with her foot. "Where's your glove?" she asked.

"I was thinking we could play something else."

Mae kicked the basketball to Jimmy Mac. "Something else?"

"Yeah," Jimmy Mac answered. "Don't you ever get tired of baseball?"

"No."

Jimmy Mac sighed. "We could try basketball for a change."

Mae beat Jimmy Mac in every sport, including darts and horseshoes.

"Have you been practicing or something?" Mae asked.

Jimmy Mac grinned big. "Maybe."

"One game of PIG," Mae said. "Then you're pitching to me." Jimmy Mac took off, and Mae picked up her bat and raced ahead of him.

Heat seeped through their sneakers on the basketball court's blacktop. It was the second week of summer, and the sun was already blazing hot in southern Georgia.

Jimmy Mac tossed the basketball to Mae. She dribbled it effortlessly between her legs. She stood behind Jimmy Mac and took a shot. It went in the basket. "Nothing but net," she said.

"Not bad," Jimmy Mac said.

Mae retrieved the ball and sent him a hard chest pass. He stood to the side of the goal and tossed the ball. It hit the rim and came back hard, ricocheting off his head.

"I thought you said you'd been practicing?" Mae said, running after the ball.

"You've got four inches on me." Jimmy Mac was on the short side and worried he'd already reached his maximum height at the end of fifth grade.

"Quit making excuses." Mae shot the ball against the faded backboard, and it went in. "Use the backboard."

"It won't help any," Jimmy Mac said. "You'll just beat me at basketball too. Let's go on to the river."

Mae held the ball on her hip and looked past Jimmy Mac. "How about a game of dodgeball first?"

"Huh?" he asked.

Mae pointed with her head. "Don't look now, but trouble's coming."

Jimmy Mac turned around and saw Bubba Duncan. Ever since the dodgeball incident, Bubba had committed to torturing Mae whenever he got the chance. They were in the same class each year, and it seemed with each added grade, Bubba multiplied his meanness toward Mae—sometimes even saying ugly things about her sister.

Bubba walked onto the blacktop and barged between the two friends. "Well, if it ain't Patch and her Tiny Mac," he said, chewing on a toothpick.

"Hey, Bubba," Jimmy Mac said. He mouthed, "Don't," to Mae.

Bubba looked around, pretending he was searching for somebody. "Where's your freaky sister?"

Mae balled up her fist and took a step closer to Bubba. Jimmy Mac leaned toward Mae and whispered, "Ignore him," under his breath.

Mae saw Jimmy Mac's fingers twitching by his side, so she took a step back. More than anything she wanted to punch Bubba in the stomach. But she also knew once she'd hit him, she'd have to take off faster than a Greyhound. And, well, Jimmy Mac was more of a Chihuahua. She couldn't very well leave him to fend for himself.

"I'm glad you're here," she said.

Jimmy Mac sighed loudly.

"Yeah?" Bubba asked.

"Yep, I heard the Wiggly's looking for a new mascot. You should apply."

Jimmy Mac shook his head. Comparing Bubba to a giant pig wasn't exactly ignoring his name-calling.

"You're funny, Mae," Bubba said. He'd chewed his toothpick down to the nub and spat it near her foot. "You think Dr. Heery could make you another patch? One to cover your entire face?"

Bubba and Mae commenced a stare-off, both making snarled faces at each other. Jimmy Mac looked at Mae, then Bubba. It was like he was watching a game of ping-pong. Mae faked like she was going to throw the basketball at Bubba, but he didn't flinch.

"Where you headed?" Jimmy Mac asked, trying to break the tension.

Bubba shifted a stink eye to Jimmy Mac. "What's it to you, Tiny Mac?"

"We're going to the river to cool off," Jimmy Mac said, his voice cracking on the "cool off" part. Mae elbowed him hard.

"Hope Mae drowns," Bubba said as he started walking away.

Mae aimed the basketball at the back of Bubba's head, and Jimmy Mac put up both hands to block it. Bubba reached the opposite edge of the blacktop and kept walking. Jimmy Mac dropped his arms.

Mae slammed the ball at the basket's rim.

"That'll be a P for you," Jimmy Mac said with a grin.

"That don't count." She looked for Bubba, but he was already out of sight. Mae cocked her head. "Something's wrong. We ain't never gotten rid of him so quick before."

Jimmy Mac craned his neck to make sure Bubba was good and gone. "He's probably getting friends to help pummel us," he said.

"Bubba ain't got no friends." Mae threw him the ball.

"He don't need any. He can do a ton of damage all by himself." He moved to the free throw line.

"I see you're stepping it up a notch," Mae said, impressed he'd moved farther from the goal. He aimed the ball at the basket. And missed by a mile. "Just a little off," she said.

Mae ran after the ball and got into position for a three-pointer.

"Maybe it's time to patch things up with Bubba." As soon as the word "patch" left his mouth, Jimmy Mac wished he could take it back. "Work things out with him, I mean."

Mae tucked the ball under her arm. "I think the heat's getting to you. You're going soft."

"It's just—I kinda feel sorry for him."

"For Bubba Duncan?"

"Yeah. He's dirt poor, and he ain't got no daddy." Jimmy Mac was familiar with that last part. He had a daddy, but he was gone a lot. After Jessup's one and only factory closed, Jimmy Mac's daddy and Mae's daddy were among the seventy-eight people out of work. Mae's daddy switched places with her mama by staying home and taking care of Shelby while her mama got a job at the grocery store. Jimmy Mac's daddy took a job on an oil platform in the middle of the Gulf of Mexico. He worked eleven months straight, coming home only for Christmas.

Bubba's daddy wasn't coming home at Christmas. Or ever. He had been killed by a train right before Bubba was born. Bubba Senior thought he could race across the tracks before the train got to him. He was wrong.

Mae spun the ball on her index finger. "When Bubba Duncan starts being nice to me, I'll start being nice to him. Maybe."

"You can't keep people on your hate list forever," Jimmy Mac said. "My mama says hate will bore a hole in your heart like a steady drip of rain."

"Bubba ain't got a heart neither."

"I wasn't talking about Bubba."

"Hey, Jimmy Mac," somebody yelled in a sing-song voice.

"What's *she* doing here?" Mae asked.

"Shh, Mae," Jimmy Mac whispered. "Hey, Savanna."

The girl rode her bicycle onto the court and stopped in front of Mae. Savanna straddled the bar on her bike and planted her two-inch wedge sandals on the blacktop.

"Hel-low, Mae," she said, her face looking like she was scraping gum off her shoe.

"Wanna shoot some hoops?" Jimmy Mac asked.

Mae locked her arms around the ball and rolled her eyes. *Pu-leeze*, Mae thought. *That uppity girl don't know what a hoop is.*

"No thanks. Grandmother is taking Mother and me shopping. In Atlanta. We're going to spend the night at the

Hyatt, then hit the mall. You know, start the back-to-school shopping early."

"Don't let us hold you up," Mae said, throwing the ball to Jimmy Mac. He didn't know it was coming until it hit him hard in his gut. He grunted.

"Maybe I'll see you when I get back to Jessup," Savanna said, pedaling away.

"Sure," he squeaked, still holding his stomach.

Mae watched Savanna's pink hair ribbons fly behind her perfectly braided ponytail like they were trying to catch up to her. "She likes you," Mae said.

"No, she doesn't."

"Yes, she does."

"Do you want to finish PIG or argue?" Jimmy Mac asked.

"Can't we do both?"

Jimmy Mac moved a few feet from the goal, held the ball between his knees, and threw up a granny shot. It surprised both of them when the ball went in the basket.

Mae moved to the same spot.

"Sorry about yesterday," Jimmy Mac said. "Your birthday party getting ruined."

Mae looked at the basket. She tossed the ball.

"Shelby okay?" he pressed.

The ball hit the rim and bounced off. She'd missed a granny shot. "I'll see you around," Mae said, picking up her baseball gear.

"Hang on," he called after her. "We don't have to talk about it." Jimmy Mac had forgotten the first rule of being Mae's friend: don't ask about her sister.

CHAPTER THREE

The screen door slammed behind Mae.

"Mae Ellen! Your daddy's resting." Her mama stood in the kitchen in her pink polyester uniform. "He's got one of his migraines," she said.

"Sorry, Mama." Mae got a glass from the cabinet and filled it with water from the faucet.

"Help with Shelby, okay? I don't get off until late."

Mae nodded and set the glass on the counter. Her mama gave her a quick squeeze. "Be sweet," she called and headed out the door.

Mae walked into the living room and crouched beside her sister. "Who's winning?" Mae turned to the TV. The Atlanta Braves were playing the Florida Marlins. "We need a win. The Fish won last night."

The sound of the crowd grew as a player knocked one out of the park. Shelby stomped her foot on the hardwood floor. She held her hands an inch apart and clapped, missing sometimes. Mae wanted to believe that Shelby knew exactly what was happening in the game, but she always responded to loud noises.

Mae smiled. "You bring them good luck, Shelby Grace. I told Daddy he should've let you stay up last night for those extra innings."

Shelby watched the Braves, the Weather Channel, and the boxed DVD set of *The Three Stooges* their daddy had bought at a truck stop. Mae shared Shelby's love of the Braves, and she got her sister's enjoyment from watching the Stooges. But the Weather Channel baffled her. There was something about the Doppler radar and talk of storms that held Shelby's attention.

Mae looked into her sister's eyes. She'd give anything to know what was going on inside Shelby's head. The doctor had said she'd likely never be able to do things like other kids, even other kids with cerebral palsy. But Mae knew her brain was always thinking. She held onto a tiny bit of hope that deep down inside, Shelby knew Mae loved her no matter what. Even if Mae sometimes complained they couldn't go places on account of it was too hard to take Shelby and her wheelchair. And even if Mae took off to the river when things got scary.

She wondered if Shelby remembered that awful day two years ago. Mae remembered it like it was yesterday. It was Shelby's worst seizure yet.

Their mama, tired from a twelve-hour shift at the grocery store, had decided to take a hot bath. Mae's job was to watch her sister while their daddy drove up the street to the Burger

Barn for an order of cheeseburgers and fried pickles. "Thirty minutes, tops," he'd told Mae, wanting to surprise his wife with dinner.

Mae and Shelby had sat watching TV until Mae decided to take a quick spin on her bike—the bike she'd just gotten for her ninth birthday.

She'd only ridden four circles in the front yard. Then she'd come back inside and found Shelby on the floor, seizing.

Mae stood frozen on the living room rug as their mama walked into the room wearing her bathrobe, hair wrapped in a towel. "Mae, call 911!" she screamed.

But Mae couldn't move. Her mama gently slid a pillow under her sister's head and looked at her watch to time the seizure. Shelby's body twitched like she'd been struck by a lightning bolt.

Her daddy ran in and dropped their dinner. A few minutes later the ambulance arrived, and her daddy waved the paramedics inside. "We used all of her rescue medicine last time," her daddy said. James knelt on the floor by Shelby as Ricky dug inside his black bag. He pulled out a container and sprayed medicine into Shelby's nose.

Mae saw her sister's blue lips. "Shelby!" she shouted.

"Shhh now," her daddy said.

She looked at him for reassurance but only saw fear in his face. She followed her mama's gaze to Shelby's blueish-purple fingers.

James slipped a mask over Shelby's nose and mouth and squeezed the attached bag in steady pumps. Ricky counted,

"One, two, three," and they lifted her onto a stretcher and began to roll her out the door.

Mae grabbed Ricky's arm. "No! Wait!" she screamed. Her daddy grabbed her and held her tight. Tears streamed down Mae's face as the birthday wish she'd made swirled inside her head, telling her it was all her fault.

Do you remember that day, Shelby? Mae thought, wondering if her sister could hear what she was thinking— if she could see inside her heart. Mae had thought about it every day for the past two years. The memory would pop up; she'd push it down. Up. Down.

A drop of drool ran down Shelby's chin, and Mae used the bottom of her own shirt to wipe it off. Shelby's eyes shifted slowly and locked with Mae's. It was like she could see all the things Mae wanted to keep hidden.

Mae blinked away a tear. She patted her sister's arm. "It's gonna be a hot summer, Shelby Grace." Mae stood and pulled back the curtains. She opened a window, and a gentle breeze blew in like a whisper.

She walked down the hall and tapped on her parents' bedroom door.

"Daddy, are you asleep?" Mae asked softly, walking into the darkened room.

"No, Mae Ellen. Just resting. Is your mama gone?"

"Yes, sir."

"I'm getting up. What do you and your sister want to eat?"

"I can fix us something. You rest, and I'll take care of Shelby tonight," she offered.

Mae's daddy slowly rose from the bed and patted down his hair. "I got it. What about breakfast for dinner?"

"Okay, as long as we can have dinner for breakfast in the morning," she answered. Mae followed her daddy out of the room.

When they reached the kitchen, she saw a thin smile brighten his tired face. "You got me thinking. How about dessert for dinner?" he asked. He held up his pinky finger, and Mae grabbed it with hers.

"I pinky swear I won't tell Mama," she said.

For two days straight, it rained hard. Mae stayed indoors and played checkers and Monopoly with her daddy and sister. Each took turns moving the checkers and top hat for Shelby.

When the sun finally peeked out from behind the clouds, Mae hit the pavement. She rode hard and fast for two miles, waited for the traffic light to turn green, and rode another mile until she got to the grocery store.

She walked inside the Piggly Wiggly and was met with enough "Hey, Mae's" you'd have thought she was the mayor. She waved to her mama, who was behind the Courtesy Counter, counting out change to a customer.

Mae headed straight for the bakery, hanging a left at Aisle 6. She saw her friend, Miss Fannie, standing behind the glass case loaded with cakes, cookies, and shiny doughnuts. She also spotted Savanna's mother, so she stayed back.

Miss Fannie placed both hands on the counter. "I'm sorry you weren't happy with my cupcakes, Mrs. Weatherall, but I swear on my Granny G's grave, they were not undercooked."

"Now, Fannie," Savanna's mother started. She pushed her designer handbag up to her shoulder and shifted her shopping basket to the other arm. "There's no need to get all bent out of shape. All I'm saying is you might want to calibrate your oven temperature."

"All *I'm* saying is nobody in this town ever complains about my baking." Miss Fannie pursed her lips. "'Cept you."

"And while we're on the subject of improvements—" Mrs. Weatherall continued, but Miss Fannie had moved down the counter, wiping it clean. "Cupcakes look much more polished when one uses foil liners," Mrs. Weatherall said. She followed Miss Fannie, thinking she might actually be interested in her suggestions. "The paper ones look unprofessional."

"Mm-hmm," Miss Fannie said.

Mrs. Weatherall looked at her watch. "Look at the time. I'd better scoot or I'll be late picking up Savanna. She has a double session now that she's in the advanced dance class."

"Better not keep her waiting." Miss Fannie dipped a plastic spoon into a tub and scooped out a spoonful of icing. She placed the spoon inside a baggie and sealed it.

Savanna's mother spun around on her heels. "Mae Moore, it's not nice to sneak up on people."

"I wasn't sneaking," Mae said. Mrs. Weatherall's eyes traveled from the crooked part in Mae's hair to her untied shoes. "I was listening to you and Miss Fannie talk cupcakes while standing over there." Mae pointed to the shelves of spaghetti sauce. "And now I'm over here."

Mrs. Weatherall frowned, then turned to Miss Fannie. "I'll be back tomorrow for my order. And remember, foil liners."

Miss Fannie gave her a wave, only it wasn't a hey-there kind of wave, but a scoot-along-now kind of wave.

Mae stepped up to the bakery glass. "Morning, Miss Fannie."

"Where've you been, Mae Ellen?" Miss Fannie flicked away crumbs from the top of her apron. "Two days straight, I had to eat cookies that had your name on 'em."

"How 'bout you give me three cookies right now?" Mae said. "It'd even things out."

Miss Fannie cackled, showing the wide black space where her front teeth should've been. She caught herself and pressed her lips together to hide the gap.

Miss Fannie pulled out a square of wax paper from the box. "I might better give you just one since it's still early. I'm hoping the rest of these get bought up before we close today."

Mae stared like she was in a trance as Miss Fannie picked up a cookie from the silver baking tray, wrapped it in the paper, and handed it to her. Chocolate-chocolate chip cookies were her specialty. They deserved two "chocolates" because Miss Fannie's recipe started with chocolate cookie dough and ended with a load of chocolate chips. Mae took a bite of the warm, gooey, chocolaty goodness. "Mank mew, Manny," she said with a mouthful of cookie.

"Baby, I love how you love my cookies," Miss Fannie said. She leaned over the glass counter and watched Mae savor each bite, then lick her fingers. "Whenever I'm feeling low, you lift me right up."

"You feeling low because of Savanna's mama?" Mae asked.

"Heavens no. I don't let anything that woman says bother me." Miss Fannie lifted a freshly frosted cake into a white box. "I'm gonna have to find me another job." She folded the top and slid the corners into curved slits.

"You can't leave the Wiggly," Mae whined. Mae knew she'd miss Miss Fannie as much as her cookies.

"Not leave. Another job in *addition* to this one here." Miss Fannie hung her head. "I got more week than paycheck."

"Oh. Money worries," Mae said. Her family had those too. Her mama's car had stopped running before school got out, and they didn't have enough cash to fix it. Sometimes her daddy had to run her mama to work, take Shelby to her doctor's appointments, and then pick up her mama at the end of her shift.

"I might lose my place," Miss Fannie added.

"Your trailer?" Mae asked. "Where would you go?"

Miss Fannie lifted her head. "Don't you worry about it none. These are grown-up problems," she said, sounding like she'd shoved all her troubles into a closet. "Tell you what, I'm gonna give you one more cookie on account of you being my best customer."

Mae reached over the counter and took it. "Miss Fannie, you should sell your cookies after store hours. You'd have more customers and money than you'd know what to do with."

Miss Fannie put her hand on her chest, and her eyes softened. "Thank you for believing in me, Mae Ellen."

Mae worried Miss Fannie might cry. She was trying to help her feel better, not worse.

Miss Fannie took a Sharpie pen and wrote "Shelby Grace" on the baggie that contained the spoonful of icing.

"Cream cheese and butter?" Mae asked.

"Mm-hmm." Shelby loved Miss Fannie's icing as much as Mae loved her cookies. A few years ago, Shelby refused to eat. It was Miss Fannie's idea to put a dab of icing in her oatmeal, smashed meatloaf, or whatever they needed to get into her stomach. It got her right back to eating.

"You heading home?" Miss Fannie asked. Mae shook her head.

"All right then. I'll give it to your mama." Miss Fannie waved a dish towel at Mae. "Now, you run on outta here. Mrs. Weatherall has probably already complained to Mr. Adams about me. He'll be here any minute to help me smooth out my customer service." Miss Fannie smiled. "Come back tomorrow, though."

"I will," Mae said.

Mae held the cookie close to her side as she passed the store manager. "Morning, Mr. Adams," she said, looking past him.

"Good morning, Mae Ellen," he said. Mr. Adams straightened the boxes of mac and cheese on a high shelf. She didn't want him to see the cookie in case it might remind him that he needed to have a talk with Miss Fannie. Mae's mama was always saying things like you can catch more flies with honey. Mae knew it had something to do with being nicer to people, but who wanted to catch flies?

Mae waited until she got to the bench outside to eat the cookie. She stuffed the entire thing in her mouth. A tall glass of cold milk would go perfectly with Miss Fannie's cookie, but she'd settle for a drink from the soda fountain machine in the deli. She started to go back in and ask her mama for some change when someone yelled, "I don't know why I even bothered coming back!"

Mae looked in both directions to see where the hollering was coming from.

"I was wondering the very same thing!" A female voice said this time. "They shoulda left your butt in jail!"

The noise came from the parking lot on the side of the grocery store. A couple's squabble wasn't any of Mae's business, but she was dying to know whose backside should've been left in jail.

A girl in high heels marched straight to her car parked in front of the Piggly Wiggly. It was Ashley. Mae knew Ashley from when she'd worked as a cashier last summer. Mae also recognized her because she was known as Davis Hampton's girlfriend.

She used to brag all over town how, once Davis signed his baseball contract, they'd get married and move to Buckhead, an expensive area in Atlanta. The first time Mae had heard her bragging, she thought Ashley had said, "Butthead." Mae laughed all day until her daddy corrected her thinking. Sometimes he could ruin a good thing.

Ashley slammed her door and drove off like she was the lead car in the Daytona 500.

Mae stood and threw her trash away.

THUNK!

She licked the last chocolate smudge off her fingers.

THUNK!

It was louder this time.

Mae couldn't ignore the mysterious noise, so she walked to the side of the store where the yelling had come from.

THUNK!

Davis Hampton, the once baseball star and pride of Jessup, sat on the hood of his dented Chevy truck with a tennis ball in his hand. He threw it hard against the side of the store, like he was trying to drill a hole into the bricks. *THUNK!* The ball bounced back to him, and he caught it without moving his hand even a fraction of an inch from where he released it.

Mae watched him throw and catch. Throw and catch. When he finally realized somebody was watching, he turned toward her.

Davis didn't look anything like he did when he left for the Big Leagues. His whiskers were now thick and black, and his hair was unwashed and longer than his ears. Dark circles surrounded his eyes like he hadn't slept in weeks. The signature cocky smile was definitely missing.

"Davis Hampton?" Mae asked.

"Yeah," he said, snarling like a mean dog.

Mae swallowed hard, afraid he might drill the ball her way.

"You Gary Moore's kid?" he asked.

"One of 'em," she answered.

Davis threw the tennis ball again. She followed the ball as it hit the nose of the pig painted on the side of the store alongside the words, "Local Since Forever."

"Can I help you?" he asked, bugging his eyes out like he was highly annoyed. "Do you want an autograph or something?"

Mae thought about it. At one time a genuine Davis Hampton autograph would have been worth something. A rookie with the Atlanta Braves on his way to a promising baseball career. But now?

"Nope," she answered.

He snickered. "So, you've heard, huh?"

"What? That you hurt your back, got hooked on drugs, and got arrested? Folks at the Wiggly said you spent only one night in jail on account of you had a good lawyer."

"Wow, news travels fast," he said, sliding off the hood of his truck. "Bad news anyway."

"So it's true? You blew a chance to get *paid* to play base-ball?" Mae asked.

"You don't mince words, do ya?"

Mae shrugged her shoulders. She wasn't sure what "mince" meant, but she figured it was related to the time the principal gave her two days of detention for having a fresh mouth. And by "fresh," he didn't mean her breath was minty clean.

Davis got in his truck and started the engine. He inched the Chevy close to Mae and leaned out his window. A tiny speck of chocolate dotted the corner of his mouth—the kind you got from eating one of Miss Fannie's cookies. He tossed her the tennis ball and put his sunglasses on.

"Maybe they'll take you back," she yelled. "If you clean up your act." He was already out of the parking lot before she finished hollering.

It was unlikely a player would get a second chance at a baseball career. Mae knew that, but she still said it. If there was one thing Mae couldn't stand, it was a hopeless situation. It didn't matter if it was Davis Hampton blowing his chance at making his dream come true, or Miss Fannie not having enough money to pay her bills, or Mae longing for assurance that her sister knew Mae loved her—no matter what she could or couldn't do.

The last thing might never happen, but maybe somebody in this tiny town could have a happy ending. All it would take was a little faith.

If only she could find some.

CHAPTER FOUR

The afternoon sun was hot enough to fry a pickle on the sidewalk, so Mae headed for the river to cool off. Once there, she'd take her shoes and socks off and wade in the water.

She pedaled fast and reached the four-way stop where she'd made her detour days earlier. Mae remembered the steep hill she'd climbed before but never coasted down. She'd seen the sign for drive-thru prayer that day and turned around.

This way. The voice was back and urging her toward and up the hill.

Mae figured it wouldn't shut up until she'd done what it said. *All right, let's see what all the fuss is about,* she said to herself.

Trees lined both sides of the road, offering shade every yard or so with their branches. The tops of her legs ached as she pedaled. The higher she went, the harder it was.

She reached the top of the hill and surveyed the downward slope. *This better be worth it,* she thought. Mae gave a kick with her foot, then pulled up both feet, resting them on the handlebars. She was flying fast.

Hopewell Church was at the bottom. Her family had been members once, but it was a long time ago. As she got closer, she saw a bike parked at an orange cone. It looked like Jimmy Mac's bicycle—red seat, silver crossbar, and black handlebars. Then she saw Floyd Foster, the preacher, sitting in a lawn chair under a big oak tree. He was talking to a little kid. As she coasted closer, she saw the little kid was Jimmy Mac.

Mae dropped her feet back on the pedals and turned off the road, steering the bike behind a thick cluster of trees. She laid her bike down and peeked through the branches. She was too far to hear what they were saying. Whatever it was, it looked serious.

Mae wondered why Jimmy Mac was talking to Preacher Floyd. If he were still a Boy Scout, he might've been selling him a canister of popcorn. But his mama made him quit when she learned he'd used a pocket knife on a camping trip. Jimmy Mac was all thumbs, and she'd been afraid he'd accidentally cut his arm off.

Then Mae realized it was Thursday—drive-thru prayer day. But she was Jimmy Mac's best friend. If he had a problem big enough to get God involved, why hadn't he told her?

He and the preacher shook hands, and Jimmy Mac walked toward his bike. Mae panicked. She couldn't let him see her—it'd look like she was spying on him.

Mae walked her bike farther into the woods and waited for him to ride by. He was slower than molasses climbing up a brick wall. Instead of riding his bike, he was walking it back up the hill.

Mae got itchy from the thickets scraping against her leg. She reached down to scratch and knocked her bike over. Jimmy Mac stopped and looked into the woods. She froze in her bent-over position and held her breath. Sweat rolled off Mae's forehead and landed on a leaf stuck in her laces. She lifted her eyes and watched as Jimmy Mac wiped his cheek with his sleeve. Then he turned back to the road and continued his snail-like pace. At the top of the hill, he climbed on his bike and rode off.

Mae was soaked in sweat, and she needed the coolness of the river now more than ever. Riding all the way down the hill could wait. She'd seen what was at the bottom, and she didn't have anything to say to Preacher Floyd.

———

Mae parked her bike at the south side of the Chattahoochee River and slid down the embankment to the water's edge. The Hooch, as the locals called it, ran through parts of Tennessee, Georgia, and Alabama. It varied from ankle deep in some places to over your head in others. The narrowest place to cross had rocks with slimy green moss growing over them.

Once, on a dare, a seventh grader crossed at an especially slippery part. She got halfway, lost her balance, and ended up with a cast from her fingers to her shoulder. Another time a teenager got swept up in the current. He would have drowned if he hadn't latched onto a low-hanging branch until his friends could pull him out.

Mae knew how to navigate each rock in order to get to the other side, but because of the recent heavy rains, the current was flowing quicker than usual. The storm had added at least two inches to the water's depth, and Mae's usual stepping rocks were almost completely submerged.

Mae leaned against a tree for balance and removed her shoes and socks. She slowly inched her right foot in, felt the cool rushing water, and stepped on her first rock. She stepped to the second one with her other foot and held her arms out wide like she was walking over Niagara Falls on a tightrope. As she placed her foot on the next slimy rock, she slipped. Mae quickly shifted her weight back and recovered her balance. She tried again, this time placing her foot on the wider part of the rock. Three more steps, and she leaped to the riverbank.

She sat on the opposite side of the Hooch, her heart slowing down to match the rhythm of the water. She tilted her head toward the sky, closed her eyes, and felt the sunlight filtering through the trees warm her face.

Mae thought about all the possible worries Jimmy Mac might have. There was his shortness for one. It had plagued him ever since Tommy Fairly, the shortest kid at Walnut Grove Elementary School, gained half an inch on him in the third grade. Then there was his daddy. His job was dangerous—working ten stories high over the ocean, drilling for oil. Or maybe it was his noticeable deficiency of any athletic ability. He could definitely use some divine intervention in that department.

She wondered where Jimmy Mac was. Once he didn't see her at the school's field, he'd know to come to the Hooch. It was his preferred meeting place since nobody kept score there. Of course, if they had cell phones, they could save themselves some pedaling. But neither was getting one of those. Both of their parents had read the school counselor's newsletter on the dangers of social media and cell phones in general. They'd made a parental pact of no phones until their kids were fourteen.

Soon Mae's mind drifted, and she began doodling in the sand with a stick.

"Phew-wee. Something sure stinks out here," somebody yelled. Mae looked up. Bubba stood on the other side of the river.

"What are you doing here?" Bubba asked. "Besides stinkin' up the place."

"None of your business!" Mae yelled back.

Bubba inched closer to the river's edge. "Try sayin' that to my face," he shouted. He looked at the water rippling over the rocks and stepped back.

"Cross on over, and I will," she said, standing as if she were protecting her land.

"Where's your Tiny Mac?" Bubba asked.

There was no way Mae was going to explain that Jimmy Mac had been detained on account of his prayer request, which somehow took precedence over Mae's and his standing appointment almost every afternoon in the summer.

"It's just you and me, Bubba. Let's settle this like sixth graders. You did get promoted to the sixth grade, didn't you?"

"Shut up, Mae!" Bubba picked up a rock and threw it at her. Mae moved her head at the very second it whizzed by. "And it ain't just you and me," Bubba said. "I brought my cousin, Beecher."

A big kid, almost the exact height and size as Bubba, stepped through the trees and stood beside him. He had blond, curly hair and a face full of freckles, just like Bubba.

Mae stretched her neck to get a better look.

"How do," Bubba Number Two called as he waved to Mae. "I'm from Villa Rica."

"Welcome to Jessup, Beecher. Sorry you're related to our least favorite resident," Mae said. Sure, she could hate the new kid just because he was kin to Bubba, but it wasn't his fault. Mae knew you couldn't pick your family members any more than you could pick your teacher. You got who you got.

"Thanks," Beecher hollered. "I'm staying with Bubba for a few weeks while my mama has my baby sister." Bubba said something to his cousin, but she couldn't hear it. Most likely it was something like, "Don't talk to the enemy, or I'll punch you in the arm."

And then Bubba punched his cousin in the arm.

"I'm Mae." Only family, Miss Fannie, and teachers on the first day of school called her by her full name, Mae Ellen.

Bubba butted in, "Yeah, her real name is Mae *Smellin'*." Bubba laughed.

"You coming over here or ain't ya?" Mae asked, wanting to get him back on topic.

Bubba moved forward and searched for a flat rock where he could place his foot. He kept his shoes on. Big mistake. There was nothing slipperier than a sneaker sole on a moss-topped rock.

His shoe slipped, and he pulled his foot back onto the sandy shore.

"Aw, you're too chicken," Mae called.

"Who you callin' chicken?" Bubba asked.

Mae sat down and resumed her doodling. "There's no way you're gonna cross the Hooch."

"How much you wanna bet?" he asked. Bubba's cousin got a front row seat on a big tree that had fallen years ago. "Tell you what—if I make it across, you'll carry my lunch tray to the table, open my milk carton, and stick a straw in it when we get back to school," Bubba said.

"That's it?" Mae asked.

"No. Then you have to say, 'Is that all, sir?' for one whole week."

"Okay, and when you *don't* cross over, you'll have to decorate your wagon, hitch it to your bike, and pull me around town like I'm queen for a day—like a parade float. Deal?"

"Deal," he said.

That was the stupidest bet I ever made, thought Mae. Getting pulled around by Bubba Duncan might be what you got if you lost a bet. But it was too late to take it back.

Bubba carefully set his foot on the nearest rock. He placed his other foot on another rock only two inches from the first one. At this pace, it'd be Thanksgiving before he made it to the other side.

"Once you get over there, you'll have to cross back over to get home in time for supper," Beecher said. He was definitely the smarter of the two.

"Shut your pie hole—I'm concentrating!" Bubba said as he took another step, and then another. He was halfway and must have felt pretty confident because he took his eyes off his feet and looked at Mae. "Just so you know, I drink three milks with my lunch." As he said "—unch," his foot slipped off the rock. He looked like one of the Stooges slipping on a banana peel. Both feet flew in the air, and he landed on his big rump. Mae laughed out loud, and so did Beecher.

Bubba tried to get his footing, but the current pushed him farther down the river.

"You better stand up before you get to deep water," she hollered.

"What do you think I'm trying to do?" Bubba yelled, struggling to get his feet under him. He was moving fast. He reached out and grabbed a twig sticking in the sand, but as he did, it snapped.

This wasn't funny anymore.

"You better do something," Mae yelled at Bubba's cousin.

"I can't swim," Beecher said, his face white with fear.

Mae ran down the side of the river, past where Bubba was floating. Her heart was racing. *Keep calm. Keep calm,* she repeated to herself.

"Help him!" Beecher screamed.

She stepped on the first rock, then hopped to another. "Grab onto something until I can get to you!" Mae yelled. She leaped like a bullfrog hopping across lily pads until she could almost reach out and touch Bubba.

When he saw her closing in, Bubba got a guilty grin on his face. The closer Mae came, the bigger the grin got. As she stretched her arm to grab hold of him, he swiped her legs under the water. Mae fell hard, hitting her shoulder on a rock. "Ow!" she shouted.

Bubba pulled his feet under him and stood. The water came to just above his knees. "Gotcha!" he shouted. Mae tried to stand, but she moved too fast and slipped on a rock. She was back on her butt when Bubba splashed water in her face.

Mae kicked hard to splash him back, but he'd already turned around and headed to shore. She wanted to scream at him, find a rock to hurl at him. How could he joke about something like dying?

Mae wanted to yell at Beecher, too, for doing absolutely nothing, but she saw him bent over, breathing hard. He had been as worried as she was that Bubba was going to drown right before their eyes.

"Did you see her face?" Bubba asked his cousin, laughing. Bubba stood on the riverbank and looked back at Mae. "Like she swallowed an ugly pill or something."

Beecher, still breathing hard, chuckled slightly.

When Mae finally stood, she brushed her hair out of her face and yelled, "Whatever! You still owe me a parade, Bubba Duncan!"

"Come on, let's go," Beecher said.

"Yeah." Bubba turned and walked behind his cousin. "There's nobody here worth seeing."

"A bet's a bet!" she shouted.

Beecher let go of a wispy branch, slapping Bubba in the face.

"Dang it, Beecher!" he yelled.

Beecher looked past his cousin and gave Mae a tiny wave.

CHAPTER FIVE

The next morning Mae sat on the edge of the bench outside the Piggly Wiggly to de-stink before walking inside the store. The bike ride had been especially sweaty. It was only 10:30, but the thermometer on Smith's Hardware sign read ninety-two degrees.

She couldn't decide if she was madder about Bubba faking a drowning or Jimmy Mac not showing up at the river. They saw each other about every day in the summer. It was their arrangement ever since they'd turned nine.

Her forehead crinkled thinking about how he didn't come looking for her all day yesterday. Still, the fact he had a problem big enough to go to Preacher Floyd about—but not say a peep to her—drove Mae near crazy with curiosity.

"Good gosh, a'mighty! It's hot out here," Miss Fannie exclaimed as she walked out the door.

"What?" Mae asked, snapping out of her trance. "Oh, hey, Miss Fannie."

"Mae Ellen, you need to get yourself inside before you have a heat stroke."

Mae lifted her armpit to her nose and took a whiff. "I'm pretty ripe. Mama likes me to air out before coming in."

Miss Fannie nodded her head. "I'll be *over*ripe by the time I get home."

"You're leaving already?" Mae asked.

"Yep." Miss Fannie reached inside her red canvas bag with a big pig on the front. The store had given one to each worker to encourage recycling. She took out a cookie wrapped in a paper towel and handed it to Mae.

"Mr. Adams says the corporate office is asking him to find ways to save money. Unfortunately, they're cutting back my hours."

Mae shook her head.

"Seems folks don't eat as many sweets in the summer months 'cause they're trying to fit into their bathing suits." Miss Fannie fanned herself with her hand. "All I know is my paycheck is gonna be smaller in the foreseeable future."

Mae took a bite of the cookie. "Maybe you could come up with a low-calorie chocolate-chocolate chip cookie," Mae said.

They looked at each other, then both burst out laughing. Miss Fannie held her hand up to hide her missing teeth. "Low-cal and cookie don't belong in the same sentence," Miss Fannie said.

"I don't know what I was thinking." Mae stuffed the rest of the cookie in her mouth.

"Well, it ain't gonna get any cooler. I'll be seeing ya, Mae Ellen." Miss Fannie started walking down Main Street.

Mae thought about the long walk Miss Fannie had. She would eventually turn off the paved road a couple of miles from the grocery store. Then she'd walk along a dirt road for another mile or so until she reached Happy Acres Trailer Park. Mae had never been to her trailer, and she wondered how far Miss Fannie was from Bubba's.

The Wiggly's automatic doors swung open, and out walked Jimmy Mac holding a thirty-two-ounce fountain drink.

"Well, look who it is," Mae said. "Where've you been?"

"Inside cooling off," he answered. He slurped his drink. "Oh, sorry. Want some? I can go back and get a refill."

Mae was more curious than thirsty. "Where were you yesterday?"

"When?"

"I waited for you at the river," Mae said. "You never showed."

"Um."

"It musta been a hundred degrees yesterday. Why weren't you there?" Mae realized her arms were folded and her face was scrunched. If she wanted information, she needed to look less like a detective and more like Jimmy Mac's best friend. They'd known each other since the Babies Bloom Room at the church nursery. She relaxed, and Jimmy Mac sat next to her.

"I *was* at the Hooch," he said. "You didn't see me."

Mae thought, *I did see you, but it wasn't at the river.*

"When I got there, I saw you talking to Bubba and some other kid."

"Beecher," Mae interrupted. "He's Bubba's cousin."

"I hung back. You know how craz—er—mad you get when Bubba's around. I thought I might need to run get help if you started something with him."

Mae recrossed her arms and pursed her lips.

"If *he* started something," Jimmy Mac corrected.

"You were spying on me?" she asked. It hadn't been twenty-four hours since Mae had spied on Jimmy Mac outside the church.

"Not spying, looking out for. I was gonna come down to the water, but the next thing I knew Bubba was floating downstream, and you were running to save him, and I don't know, I guess I got scared." Jimmy Mac looked at the ground. He moved the dirt around with his foot.

"Then you went down, and Bubba stood up. Boy, you were madder than a hornet getting his nest kicked," he said. "It was too late to show myself then. So I waited until Bubba and—" Jimmy Mac scratched his head.

"Beecher!" Mae shouted.

"—Beecher left."

"Why didn't you say anything then?" Mae asked.

"Like I said, you looked pretty mad. Kinda like you look right now."

Mae sighed. "It's not like I needed you or anything. I was about to punch him when I slipped." She tried to read his expression to see if he knew Bubba had had the upper hand—or leg.

Jimmy Mac nodded.

Mae looked at the bike stand outside the store where her lone bike stood. "Where's your bike?"

"Got a nail in the tire when I left the chur—Hooch," he said. His face twisted up like he'd sucked a lemon.

Serves you right, she thought.

A car pulled into a parking spot close to them. It was Mae's daddy and her sister Shelby.

"Daddy's taking us for a haircut." Mae walked toward the car. She wrestled Shelby's wheelchair out of the trunk, set it on the ground, and pushed the armrests apart. "You can ride my bike home if you want," she told Jimmy Mac. No matter what he might do, Mae couldn't stay mad at him. He was her best friend. Most days, he was her *only* friend.

"Thanks!" he said. "I'll take good care of it." He tossed his empty drink cup toward the trash can but missed.

Mae's daddy lifted Shelby out of the car and gently placed her in her chair. Shelby's eyes followed Jimmy Mac as he retrieved his cup and walked it over to the trash.

He moved close to Shelby and waved. "Hey, Shelby," Jimmy Mac said. She clapped her hands and grunted. She liked him, and Mae was sure it was because he treated Shelby like any other kid.

"We better skedaddle if we're gonna make your appointment. Good to see ya, Jimmy Mac," Mae's daddy said.

"You too." Jimmy Mac got on Mae's bike. "Thanks for the loaner," he said, starting down the street.

Mae walked alongside her daddy as he pushed Shelby's chair. Just ahead, they watched Jimmy Mac get his pants' leg caught in the bike's chain. He tried to tug it loose, but it wasn't budging.

"That was a mistake," Mae groaned.

"Who wears blue jeans when it's ninety degrees?" her daddy asked.

"Chiggers and mosquitos like him. His mama's afraid he'll get bit and swell up."

Jimmy Mac yanked hard, popped the chain off the bike, and fell on the asphalt. He turned back to see if they had noticed. "I'm okay!" he said, waving.

"He's gonna destroy my only means of transportation," Mae said.

They stopped at the corner to wait at the traffic light. "Have some patience, Mae Ellen. He's just a little . . ."

"Uncoordinated?" Mae asked.

"Accident prone."

"That too."

Jimmy Mac walked the bike to the side of the street and sat on the curb so he could reattach the chain.

A truck came to an abrupt stop when the light turned red. The driver tipped his baseball cap to Mae's daddy. Her daddy nodded back, then asked, "When'd Davis get back in town?"

"A few days ago," Mae answered. They crossed the street, and Mae waited until they got to the other side to add, "Ruined his career on account of drugs."

Mae's daddy stopped on the sidewalk. "I don't think we know the whole story, Mae Ellen."

"He—" she started.

"We cheered for Davis when he was winning." Her daddy started walking again while pushing Shelby.

"Yeah, but—" she tried again.

"We wouldn't be very good friends to stop, now that he's not."

"Yes, sir." Her daddy seemed to think of Davis as a whole person, while Mae could only think of him as a star baseball player. Now that he wasn't one anymore, she wasn't sure what was left.

Mae, Shelby, and her daddy walked past Drexall's Drug Store and the Chic Boutique and arrived at Sue's Scissors Hair Salon. A bell rang as Mae pushed the door open to let her daddy wheel Shelby inside.

"I'll be right with you," Sue hollered from the back of the salon.

Mae picked up a hairstyle magazine from one of the pink plastic chairs and sat down. She heard somebody clear her throat and looked to see Savanna Weatherall sitting in one of the styling chairs. Savanna stared at Shelby, her face grossed-out as she watched Mae's daddy wipe drool off Shelby's chin with his handkerchief.

"Mother, are you about done?" Savanna asked, not taking her eyes off Shelby.

"Almost, sweetie," her mother said. She looked in the mirror and combed her bangs with her fingers. "Sue, I think we're a little uneven right here."

Mae's daddy picked up the folded newspaper from a chair and sat. He crossed his leg over his knee and began reading.

Shelby looked at the lampshade lined with white fringe and batted at it with her fingers. She laughed, watching it swing back and forth. It wasn't a regular sounding laugh— it was more like a combination of a squeal and a bark, and really loud. Mae used to get embarrassed when her sister laughed in public. She'd melt behind her daddy, hoping nobody would see her. But now Mae liked to hear her sister let the world know she was happy.

Savanna wrinkled her nose. "Can she keep it down a little?" Savanna shook her head while she punched numbers on her cell phone. "I need to make a call."

Mae jumped up and walked to the lampshade. She hit the fringe on the other side, moving her fingers fast like she was playing the piano. Shelby laughed louder and slapped her open hand on the table.

Her daddy lowered the newspaper. "Mae Ellen," he said.

Savanna stood, cell phone glued to her ear. "Mother, I'll be outside." The bell jingled as she left.

"Was that really necessary?" Mae's daddy asked.

"She's rude like that all the time," Mae whispered.

"I was talking about you, Mae Ellen," he said.

A brightly colored sign hung on the wall above Sue's cash drawer, and it caught Shelby's eye. Her sister stared at the bold black words printed on the neon-orange poster board. Mae was thankful for the distraction and followed Shelby's gaze. Mae walked closer to the poster.

"It's pretty, isn't it, Shelby?" Mae read:

PUBLIC AUCTION

THE DONUT HOLE

DIRT CHEAP

BIDDING STARTS AT 8 A.M. JULY 17TH

NO BID TOO SMALL

The Donut Hole was a doughnut and coffee shop owned by the Haynes sisters. They were in their nineties and had inherited the place from their father. There'd been a For Sale sign on the shop's doors for more than a year.

The door swung open as Savanna walked back in. She looked in one of Sue's mirrors and smoothed down her hair. She saw Mae looking at the poster and turned back around.

"They should tear the place down and start over," she said. "It was built back when only dinosaurs drank coffee."

Mae heard a tiny giggle behind her daddy's newspaper.

"Mother's thinking about putting in her own place," Savanna continued as if Mae was interested. Mae rolled her eyes.

"You know, so she can sell her peach preserves, peach muffins, peach butter, and such." Savanna opened her purse and took out lip balm. She applied it liberally.

"Oh, and peach cobbler. Mother's peach cobbler is to die for," Savanna said.

"Holy cow!" Mae said. "People actually die from eating your mother's cobbler?" Her daddy couldn't help but laugh this time.

"Honestly, Mae," Savanna said, dropping her balm in her purse. Mrs. Weatherall, finally satisfied with her hair, stood by her daughter. "We'd make a killing," Savanna said.

Mrs. Weatherall turned to Mae's daddy, "The cobbler recipe has been in our family for four generations. The secret is the peaches."

"There's peaches in peach cobbler?" Mae's daddy asked, smiling.

Savanna's mother laughed, "It's a particular kind, Gary. You know we grow the sweetest peaches in the state in our orchard."

"You do, Alice," Mae's daddy said, folding the paper. "I'm sure you'd be a huge success."

"Oh, I don't know. If I was to open up a place, I'd be better off doing it in Atlanta. This town's not making anybody any money." Mrs. Weatherall shook her head. "Still, it might be kind of fun to have my own store. I'd be sharing my talents with the community."

Mae cut her eyes to her daddy and wondered if he was thinking what she was. By "sharing my talents," Mrs. Weatherall meant charging a fortune.

"Can we go now?" Savanna asked, her lip curling. She leaned as far back from Shelby as she could while moving toward the door.

Mae opened her mouth to say something smart-alecky, but when her daddy shot her a warning look, she closed it. She turned to the poster. "Dirt cheap," she mumbled. Mae thought about Miss Fannie and how she should sell *her* treats in town. Maybe she could afford dirt cheap.

CHAPTER
SIX

For the next few days, all Mae could think about was The Donut Hole auction and how Savanna's mother said she was thinking about opening up a shop in town. It'd give Savanna more than new clothes and a perfect book bag to brag about when they started middle school in August. She pictured Savanna walking into school, telling a hallway full of giggling girls about working in the store, selling her mother's famous peach cobbler. But the worst part—a shop that sold sweets would mean competition for Miss Fannie. She had enough trouble making a living at the grocery store as it was.

Mae thought about all the times Miss Fannie had stayed with her when her parents had to be at the hospital with Shelby. Then there were all the free desserts. Mae owed Miss Fannie. It made Mae's belly sick thinking how Miss Fannie might lose her home.

Mae shifted her thinking to Jimmy Mac. That didn't make her brain hurt, until she remembered it was Tuesday and the drive-thru prayer line at the church was open. She wondered if Jimmy Mac would make a second appearance. If so, maybe she could find out why he needed prayer.

———————

The tops of Mae's thighs still ached from last week's ride, but she pressed the bike pedals hard all the way up the hill. When she made it to the other side, she hid behind the same cluster of trees and waited for Jimmy Mac.

Mae was prepared this time. She had packed a can of cola, peanut butter crackers, and the required summer reading for those going into the sixth grade, a paperback copy of *Walk Two Moons*.

She didn't have to wait long. But instead of Jimmy Mac, it was Bubba at the top of the hill. He was on his scratched-up, multi-colored bike he'd pieced together from old parts. Mae remembered driving by the junkyard once and seeing Bubba fishing through the mangled mass of old bikes. Her daddy had said, "That boy's resourceful," and Mae remembered almost feeling sorry for him. Almost.

Bubba turned his head side to side slowly, like he was making sure no one was watching. Then he placed his feet on the pedals and flew down the hill.

"Whoa! Whoa!" he screamed. Bubba's handlebars were moving all willy-nilly. Mae hushed her giggling behind the trees.

Bubba pumped the pedals backward to slow down, but it was too late. The preacher stood from his lawn chair and put his hands out. Bubba flattened the orange cone at the front of the church's driveway and nearly knocked Preacher Floyd over before he finally came to a complete stop.

Mae wiggled through the undergrowth, straining to hear what they were saying, but she was too far away. She watched Bubba kick the ground with his foot as he talked. After a few minutes, the preacher placed his hand on Bubba's shoulder and lowered his head.

A thorny vine got ahold of Mae's shoelaces. She tried to shake it free, but it wouldn't let go. She bent down and carefully removed each sharp thorn stuck to her like an octopus's tentacles. By the time she turned to look again, Bubba was trying to ride his bike back up the hill. He gave up, got off the seat, and straddled the bar. Mae watched him waddle with the bike until he was out of sight.

Mae sat on a stump close by and wondered what somebody like Bubba would pray for. Maybe it was for some smarts because nobody would walk their bike up a hill while straddling the bar.

She unloaded her drawstring backpack. She'd wrapped her drink in foil, hoping it'd stay as cold as when she took it from the refrigerator. It hadn't. But it was wet and helped wash down the crackers. She opened her book and began reading.

Almost thirty minutes passed before a pickup truck crested the hill. Mae hopped up and manned her station as Davis Hampton drove down the hill. It was obvious why he'd pay the drive-thru a visit—he had an injured back, a drug problem, and no more future in baseball. Mae wondered if he could pray for all three in a single visit or if he had to tackle each trouble, one at time.

Davis pulled up like he was ordering a strawberry milk-shake with large fries at the Burger Barn. The preacher stood by Davis's open window, his hand resting on the door of the truck and his head lowered to see in. Mae wondered if Preacher Floyd ought to get so close, given Davis's temper and all.

The preacher leaned in closer, and Mae got the feeling the visit might take a while. She wondered if Preacher Floyd was asking about famous ballplayers Davis might've played with when he was with the Braves.

Or maybe they were rehashing that high school game from a few years ago. The Jessup High School Tigers were playing for the state title. That's what Mae had wanted to ask Davis about the other day at the Wiggly when she saw him getting dumped by his girlfriend.

Everybody was in the stands that game, including a couple of MLB scouts—all there to see number 15, Davis Hampton.

Mae and her daddy were there as usual. He took off from work every home game to run the scoreboard. He'd go back to the factory once the game was over and work the late shift. It was Mae's favorite three hours—just Mae and her daddy. Uninterrupted time watching their favorite sport together. There were no money problems, no tired parents, no wheelchairs.

Mae remembered that day like it was yesterday.

Davis's shoulder was sore from the previous game, so the coach had saved him until the sixth inning. Jessup was behind, four to five. The scouts stood at the fence—their radar guns pointed at Davis.

He struck out all three batters. The ball had whizzed by each batter as they swung and missed. The other team's coach had called time and asked the umpire to check the ball for petroleum jelly or spit. When the Tigers got up to bat, they didn't score, so they were still down a run.

At the top of the seventh inning, the other team's ninth batter came up to bat, and Davis nicked his elbow on a 0 and 2 count. The visitors' bleachers went crazy, yelling Davis had hit him on purpose.

"Time!" called the umpire. "Batter, take your base." The ump walked out to the mound and motioned for Jessup's coach to join him there.

Both sides went silent, trying to hear the conversation. Davis just stared, then said something to the umpire.

"Do it again, and you're out of the game, Hampton." The ump walked back to home plate, turned to Davis, and yelled, "I don't care how many scouts are here to see ya."

Folks debated for weeks if Davis had intentionally hit the batter. It wasn't completely out of the realm of possibility. Davis had a temper.

Once, Davis had run full speed into a first baseman, knocking him off his feet. He'd gotten himself ejected that time, and the Tigers lost the game. Mae's daddy had once said, "Davis's temper is not his friend," then he'd looked at Mae, hoping she'd get the hint.

But Mae and her daddy knew the truth—the batter had crowded the plate, wanting to get hit for a walk. They could see it perfectly from their seat behind home plate in the scorebox.

On the next pitch, the runner stole second base. Davis slapped his leg with his glove. He should have checked the runner before pitching the ball. His next pitch was a knuckler that went wild. The runner was already standing on third base by the time the catcher could get the ball that had rolled to the backstop.

"Calm down, Davis," Mae had heard her daddy whisper.

The Tigers' coach called time and trotted to the mound. He said something to Davis, then put up two fingers motioning for a new pitcher to come in the game. Davis held his glove to hide his mouth and said something. The coach shuffled the dirt on the mound with his foot before waving off the new pitcher.

Mae had always wondered what Davis had said to convince the coach to change his mind. He'd left Davis in— even with another potential run on third base.

With one out, the batter popped up, and Davis struck out the next one. Tigers' fans cheered, Davis's mama cried, and Mae leaned so far out the scorebox window her daddy had to hold onto the back of her shirt so that she wouldn't fall onto the umpire.

"Way to pitch!" she'd yelled.

The Tigers were still down a run, but they had a runner on first base when Davis came up to bat. On a full count, Davis hit a rocket over the fence in right field. A walk-off home run. The Tigers won, and Davis was headed to the minors.

Mae's book slid off her lap, snapping her back to the present. That was a game worth reliving. It drove Mae bonkers that she couldn't hear what Davis and the preacher were saying, but she was as close as she could get and still be hidden by the trees.

Once Davis finally left, Mae debated sticking around to see if Jimmy Mac would show up. Maybe he wasn't coming today. Maybe he'd come and gone before she'd gotten here. There was only one way to find out.

When she reached the church, Mae parked her bike beside the bent orange cone and approached the preacher.

"Well, hello, Mae Ellen," the preacher said. He reached into a small cooler resting on the ground near his chair. He took out an ice cube, set his hat on his knee, and rubbed the ice on his bald head and the back of his neck. "It's a hot one today."

"Yes, sir, it is," she said.

"Are you here for prayer?" he asked, placing his hat back on his head.

"Not exactly."

Preacher Floyd had been the pastor of Hopewell Community Church longer than Mae had been alive. He knew Mae's family even if they hadn't been to church in a good long while.

"How's Shelby doing?" he asked.

"She's fine."

"Your mama and daddy?"

"They're good."

Preacher Floyd nodded his head and waited.

"Was that Davis Hampton I saw leaving?" she asked, taking a seat by the preacher.

"Might've been."

"And Jimmy Mac told me he came to see ya." Mae wondered if lying to a preacher was worse than lying to a regular person.

The preacher reached back into his cooler. "Care for a drink?" he asked, handing a bottle of water to her.

Mae took it, unscrewed the top, and took a big swig. She wiped her mouth with the back of her hand.

"Yeah. I'm his best friend," she said.

"Whose best friend?"

"Jimmy Mac's."

"I see."

"So if he had a problem or was worried about something or needed anything, I should probably know about it." Mae took another drink and kept her eyes on Preacher Floyd.

The preacher got another water out of the cooler and took a big gulp. "I like to put little packets of sweetened flavorings in my water, but Wanda didn't pack me any today. She prefers I drink plain H_2O."

"Jimmy Mac likes to add those sugary drink powders to his water," Mae said, trying to steer the conversation back to the reason she was there.

"You got any cherry-flavored packages in there?" he asked, pointing to her backpack.

"'Fraid not. All I had was a soft drink, and I finished it while I was—Mama says red dye makes me hyper." *That was close,* Mae thought. Mae figured if he knew she'd been spying through the trees, he'd never share Jimmy Mac's burden with her.

They sat, neither one talking. The only sounds were made by a couple of birds in the tree branches above them. Mae wondered how long it would take to get the preacher to spill the beans. He wasn't taking any of her hints, so she decided to be more direct.

"Maybe you could tell me what Jimmy Mac told you, so I could, ya know, help him out."

The preacher screwed the top on his water and set it back in the cooler. "Mae Ellen, do you know what confidential means?"

"Yes, sir, but—"

"It means private. Secret. It means not telling other people what somebody has told you."

"But I'm not 'other' people. I'm Jimmy Mac's best friend."

The preacher shook his head. "What folks tell me stays between me, them, and God."

Mae stood. "Well then, I guess I came down here for nothing."

"What about you?" he asked.

"Sir?"

The preacher pointed to a smaller version of the sign advertising drive-thru prayer on the road. The ruler stapled to the back of the sign stuck crookedly in the hard ground.

Mae thought about it. She'd said plenty of prayers. Most of them were for Shelby. For her to be healed. To be able to walk. To stay up late and tell her stories. Prayers that Shelby would know Mae loved her even if she ran off when the ambulance came. But God never answered them.

"Nope," she told the preacher. "I'm good."

"Sometimes folks come to the drive-thru 'cause they got something heavy on their heart," the preacher explained.

Mae wanted to keep her heart private. She wondered if he knew her secret—her sin. The birthday wish she'd made and hoped would stay hidden forever, or else people would know what a terrible sister she was.

Mae needed to get the preacher's nose out of her heart's business and back on somebody else's.

She thought about Miss Fannie. Maybe Mae's prayers didn't work because they were selfish. Sure, she wanted Shelby to be regular so that she could have a better life, but mainly the prayers were for Mae. So she could have a sister she could do regular sister things with. Maybe a prayer would work if it were for somebody else.

"You know Miss Fannie, right?"

"Chocolate-chocolate chip cookie Miss Fannie?" the preacher asked.

"Uh-huh."

"Indeed, I do. She attends another church, but her pastor and I are friends. We have a shared love of her cookies."

"Well, she needs help. Money-kind of help." Mae remained vague.

"I see."

"Could you pray for something good to happen to her?" Mae asked.

Preacher Floyd stood beside her and said, "Let's pray for Miss Fannie." He bowed his head and talked in a low, soft voice. Mae lowered her head and stared at the ground. When she felt the preacher was about to say "Amen," she closed her eyes tight. Peeking during a prayer might mean it wouldn't take.

"I'm glad you stopped by, Mae Ellen."

"I better get home. Daddy will wonder where I am," Mae said, retrieving her bike.

The preacher looked at his watch. "Yes, it's getting close to six. Wanda doesn't appreciate it when I'm late for supper. Tell your family 'hey' for me, okay?"

"I will." Mae started pedaling.

"And come again," he called after her.

Come again? She echoed. Mae pedaled faster. She wished she hadn't come this time. Except—it had given her an idea. Get Miss Fannie to bid on The Donut Hole before Savanna's mother did.

CHAPTER SEVEN

When Mae got up the next morning, her daddy sat at the kitchen table with her sister. "Morning, Shelby," Mae said. She watched her daddy break open a capsule and sprinkle the medicine on top of Shelby's oatmeal. He stirred it in, then slipped a spoonful of oatmeal into Shelby's mouth. "Want me to do it?" she asked him.

"No, thanks. You get yourself breakfast."

Mae opened the pantry door to find her cereal and came face to face with the calendar tacked on the inside.

"What's today?" she asked.

"Wednesday."

"No. The date."

"July 10th. Why?" her daddy asked.

"Ugh. I've got more summer behind me than I do in front of me. School will be starting soon," she groaned. Her shoulders slumped.

"What are you moaning about? Middle school was the best years of my life," her daddy said, wiping oatmeal off Shelby's chin.

"You didn't have to go to school with Savanna Weatherall."

"The world's full of Savanna Weatheralls. Folks with more passing judgment on those with less."

"Pbbbt." Shelby blew air through her lips to let her daddy know she was full or that she didn't care much for Savanna either.

"Let me see," he said, standing from the table. "Holy cow. Two more weeks and your mama and I will have been married fourteen years."

"Fourteen years?"

"Yep." He took Shelby's bowl to the sink and turned on the faucet.

Mae poured corn flakes into a bowl and doused it with milk. She sat next to Shelby. "Tell me how you and Mama met again."

Her daddy shook his head. "There's no time. Shelby's got a doctor's appointment this morning."

"Come on," Mae pleaded. Shelby slapped her hand on the kitchen table. "See, she wants to hear it too."

"You've heard it a thousand times."

"One more. Pleeeeeeze?"

He removed the paper towel tucked into Shelby's shirt collar to catch the breakfast that didn't make it into her stomach and sat down.

"We had just moved to Jessup in the fall of my senior year of high school. Grandpa Phil had gotten the job as the night supervisor at the factory. It was a horrible time to move, but at least I was there in time to try out for the baseball team."

"You were good too, weren't ya?" Mae interrupted.

"I was average." He raised his hand above his head. "This is Davis Hampton, a perfect ten." Then he lowered his hand to his knee. "And this was me—a mediocre four."

Mae knew better. She'd inherited her athletic ability from her daddy.

"On my first day, I was getting acquainted with my locker when I saw your mama in the hallway. She was beautiful." He rubbed the top of Mae's head. "Long brown hair, the color of yours and Shelby Grace's."

Mae loved being compared to her mama, but the truth was, Shelby was the spitting image of their mama, and Mae looked more like their daddy. It wasn't a bad thing, but if you had your choice between looking like Miss Georgia or looking like—well, not Miss Georgia—most folks would choose the beauty queen.

"I watched as the other kids passed her, each saying 'Hey,' and her smiling that kind smile she has."

"It was love at first sight, Shelby," Mae said, patting her sister's arm. Shelby let out a tiny sound—almost like a hum.

"Not on Leigh Ann's part. She was dating some stud on the football team, Sam Meredith." He pointed to Mae.

"Savanna Weatherall's uncle," Mae said, right on cue.

"She wore his letterman's jacket, cheered for him at the football games, rode in his expensive car—the whole nine yards. I was pretty sure she didn't even know I was alive. But one night—"

"This is our favorite part," Mae told Shelby.

"There was a school dance, and I was there by myself. Your grandma made me go."

"You don't say 'no' to Grandma Hazel," Mae said.

"You do not. Anyway, I was there. Your mama, of course, had gone with Sam."

Mae rolled her eyes. "Of course."

Her daddy smiled. "Sam had gone out to the parking lot with a bunch of his football buddies. He'd stashed beer in his car. Your mama wanted to dance, and she couldn't find her dance partner, so she went outside looking for him.

"He was loud, and he and his friends were carrying on like a bunch of idiots, throwing empty beer bottles at other cars. Your mama picked up a pebble and threw it at Sam's shiny red convertible to give him a taste of his own medicine, and he went ballistic. Called her all sorts of mean names. She told him she never wanted to see him again."

"His loss was your gain," Mae said.

Mae's daddy nodded. "When I promised my mama I'd go to the dance, I didn't promise to actually walk inside the gym. I was sitting in my car, so I'd heard and seen it all."

Mae's daddy looked at the clock above the stove. "I best hurry this up, or we'll be late. I followed your mama inside the gym. She was crying, and all of her girlfriends swarmed in to find out what had happened. A little voice inside my head said, *Go on. Ask her.*"

"We're glad you listened," Mae said.

"Me too. I walked up to her, put my hand out, and asked, 'Leigh Ann, would you care to dance?' Her friends looked me up and down and then at each other, thinking, *Who does this guy think he is?*"

"And she said, 'Yes,'" Mae said.

"She said, 'Yes.'"

"We love that story, don't we, Shelbs?" Shelby turned her head to Mae and looked her straight in her eyes. Mae liked to hear about the times when her parents were happy. Now, they just seemed tired. Mae looked at her soggy cereal. The story had been too good to eat the corn flakes while they were actually crunchy.

Her daddy got up from the table. "You know I lied earlier."

"What?"

"The best years of my life weren't in middle school. They're the years I've spent with your mama and you two."

"They're my best years too," Mae said.

"They're your only years."

"True." Mae nodded. "Tell us about getting Mama to marry you."

"Oh no, you don't. We've gotta git." He poured coffee in a travel mug. "What have you got planned for today?"

"The usual. Ride to the Wiggly. Eat a cookie—if I'm lucky, two. Sit on the bench outside until something interesting strikes me. Meet Jimmy Mac at the Hooch."

"Sounds exciting." He pulled Shelby's wheelchair away from the table.

Mae opened the front door, and her daddy grabbed his keys off the hook on the wall and pushed Shelby through.

"Bye, Daddy. Be good, Shelby. Don't kick the doctor," Mae hollered as they loaded into the car.

"I think he's safe. There won't be any finger pricks or shots this time," her daddy replied.

Mae watched as they drove down the driveway. She leaned against the porch post and thought about the rest of the story. Her daddy had gone off to junior college, but after the first year, he'd missed Mae's mama so much, he came back home and got a job at the carpet factory. When he asked her to marry him, he promised he'd buy her a big house with a white fence and a garden big enough to grow vegetables and pink roses.

Mae looked at the yard. There were two rose bushes by the house, but weeds had grown up around them and snuffed out any sign of flowers. She went back into the kitchen and looked around. White paint had chipped off the wall at the back of the sink, and the linoleum was scratched up from Shelby's wheelchair and Mae's skates. With Shelby's medical bills and her daddy losing his job, he hadn't made good on his promise.

Fourteen years, she thought. Her parents deserved some happiness. Mae ran to her room and picked up the bank on her dresser. It was a miniature Piggly Wiggly pig her mama had brought home two years ago. The store had given them away when you spent fifty dollars or more on groceries.

Mae emptied it. She ironed out a wadded-up twenty-dollar bill with her hand. She'd earned it feeding the neighbors' two wiener dogs last summer when they went to Jekyll Island. There were a couple of ten-dollar bills—birthday money—a five, a handful of ones, and a boatload of coins. It totaled $57.20. Mae wished for more, but money-making opportunities were few and far between. She'd never gotten paid for doing chores, partly because there was never extra cash lying around the Moore household and partly because she had never been what you'd call a perfect chore performer.

She wanted to do something special for their anniversary. One of Miss Fannie's special cakes? Dinner at a fancy restaurant? Mae could look after Shelby, and her parents could have a real night out.

Watch Shelby. Mae had failed so miserably at that before. But she wouldn't this time. This time she'd put Shelby's needs before her own and make up for that stupid birthday wish.

CHAPTER EIGHT

houghts flooded Mae's head as she pedaled to the Piggly Wiggly. There was planning her parents' anniversary dinner, Jimmy Mac's worry that was so big it needed prayer, and getting Miss Fannie to somehow bid on The Donut Hole so she could fix her money troubles. *So much to figure out and so little summer left,* she thought.

She walked through the automatic doors and heard her mama say, "Here ya go, Mrs. Carter, $4.50 for the ice cream." She handed the money to the lady standing at the Courtesy Counter. "Remember to take your next carton of rocky road out of the car right when you get home. This heat is a beast." Mae's mama placed the carton of melted ice cream in the trash can.

"Thank you, Leigh Ann. Sometimes I forget," said the gray-haired lady with the hunched back.

"I forget stuff all the time. Like last week when it thunder stormed—I forgot I had laundry on the line. Mae Ellen found leaves in her underwear." Both ladies laughed. Her mama spotted Mae's look of embarrassment and smiled at her.

Mae wanted to ask her mama for money for a drink. But she didn't want to get caught up in a conversation about undies hanging outside due to their dryer being on the fritz for the hundredth time.

"Good. You're still here," Mae said to Miss Fannie when she reached the bakery.

"About to close up." Miss Fannie placed an unfamiliar cookie in a box and tucked in the lid.

"Whatcha got there?" Mae asked, leaning over the glass counter.

"A baking experiment gone bad." Miss Fannie handed the box to Mae. "You can have 'em if you want."

Mae took it. The box felt full of cookies—probably a dozen. It was like winning the lottery. "Nothing you make could ever taste bad."

"They sure look like they do. Poor presentation," Miss Fannie said, shaking her head. She took off her white apron, stained with the morning's baking, and shoved it into her canvas bag.

"I want to put in a baking order," Mae said.

"Really?" Miss Fannie perked up. She grabbed her notepad and pen with the plastic yellow daisy taped to the end of it.

Mae nodded. "An anniversary cake for my parents."

"How long have they been married?"

"Fourteen years!"

"That's almost a record. Folks don't seem to stick together like they used to. Every time I pass the magazines at the check-out, I read about another break-up," Miss Fannie said.

"Uh-huh." Mae hesitated. "The problem is . . . I don't have a lot of money to spend on account of I want 'em to celebrate with a fancy dinner too."

"Oh, this one's on the house. Your mama's been nothing but kind to me. She covers for me when I need to take a break. Sometimes these ovens get so hot, I gotta step outside to breathe. And your daddy—the way he looks after Shelby Grace. This cake's my gift to them."

"Thank you, Miss Fannie."

"Now, what'd ya have in mind?" Miss Fannie asked, licking the ink part of her pen.

"Something pretty. With lots of pink roses. And cream cheese and butter icing! It's a surprise, so I want it to be perfect."

"I got just the thing. And it'll taste yummy too!"

"I know it will." Mae saw Miss Fannie's mood rise with every word she scribbled on the notepad. Now to introduce the idea of buying The Donut Hole.

"Miss Fannie, have you ever considered—"

"When did you say you needed it?" Miss Fannie had a one-track mind when it came to special orders.

"A week from Monday."

Miss Fannie wrote some more.

Mae started again, "Have you ever thought about opening your own place and selling your cookies?"

Miss Fannie looked up from her notes. "Why would I wanna do that? I can sell 'em here."

"But you could keep the money for yourself," Mae said. "You could even sell your spoonfuls of icing. Like you give Shelby."

Miss Fannie narrowed her eyes. "That's my special gift to Shelby Grace. That's for her."

Mae's shoulders slumped. "Okay. You could sell your cakes to restaurants. You could become famous."

"Famous? Girl, I ain't got no time for that. I gotta get to the cake supply store. I need a new tip for my icing bag— one for making the prettiest roses you've ever seen." Miss Fannie ripped off the top sheet of paper and stuck it in her purse. She marched toward the front of the store, and Mae could hear her mumbling words like "cake flour" and "food coloring."

Mae had never seen Miss Fannie move so fast. Mae kicked the shelf of peanut butter on Aisle 7. It seemed like Miss Fannie wasn't a bit interested in solving her money problems the way Mae had planned. She'd figured the prayer Preacher Floyd made her pray wouldn't get answered. There was no way Miss Fannie was going to make her dirt-cheap bid before somebody else did—and that somebody else was probably Mrs. Weatherall.

Her mama waved as Mae walked by, and Mae let out a big sigh. Her mama had moved to a check-out line and was ringing up groceries. Asking for drink money was still out of the question.

When Mae walked out the store's doors, someone was sitting on her bench. Well, it wasn't exactly *her* bench. Other folks sat on it, but it tended to belong to her during the hot mornings of summer. Whoever it was had a cap pulled down low over his head and wore mirrored sunglasses—the kind where you could see yourself.

Mae sat on the bench on the other side of the grocery store doors. She lifted the lid to the box of cookies, and a sweet smell escaped. Mae closed her eyes and breathed in the smells of chocolate, peanut butter, and vanilla.

She tucked the lid back in. She wanted one, but she wasn't sure about eating it in front of the stranger sitting on the other side. Mae heard him whistling softly as he bent down to tie his shoe.

She strummed the top of the box with her fingers. She thought about what her mama always said about patience being a virtue, but Mae figured if she'd lived eleven years without many virtues, she could live a little longer. Besides, as her daddy liked to say, "The early bird gets the worm,"—or in this case, cookie—and she hadn't slept in late at all this summer.

She tore open the lid and picked up a cookie. It was gooier than Miss Fannie's usual. It had globs of chocolate chunks, not chips. It wasn't the prettiest cookie she'd ever seen, but what mattered was the taste. Mae took a bite. She leaned her head back against the bench and savored the flavors.

"Didn't your mama teach you any manners?" the man on the bench asked, lifting his hat off his forehead.

The voice startled Mae until she realized who it belonged to. "Davis?"

"You get those from Miss Fannie?"

"Do chigger bites itch?" she asked.

Davis grinned. "Last I checked."

Mae walked to the other bench. No wonder she hadn't recognized him. Davis was clean-shaven, and his hair wasn't below his ears anymore. Mae held out the box. "Want one?"

"I could smell them all the way over here." Davis took one and ate it in two bites. He reached in to take another, but paused.

"Go on. I can't eat 'em all." Mae took another one for herself and sat beside him.

"Miss Fannie give you a deal on all of these or something?"

"More like she was trying to get rid of them. She wasn't happy with how they turned out."

"Miss Fannie couldn't make something taste bad if she tried. She's made my birthday cake since I was one," he said.

"Really?" Mae asked. "Mine and my sister's too."

"She made a double-layered cookie cake before each one of our games." Davis took a bite of cookie. "I think Miss Fannie is the real reason we had a winning season each year."

Davis loved Miss Fannie's baking as much as Mae did. He even owed her for his wins. He'd just said so. Maybe he'd be as dogged as Mae about helping her.

Mae scooted back on the bench. "I think she should open up her own bake shop." She wasn't sure he was listening. His eyes were locked on the cookie. "Did you know The Donut Hole was going up for auction?" she asked.

"You don't say," he answered, licking his fingers.

"Uh-huh. And I was thinking—"

Mr. Adams walked out of the store, and Mae zipped her lips. She wasn't sure how Miss Fannie's boss would feel about her opening up her own bakery.

The store manager glanced at the two of them on the bench. "Good afternoon, Mae Ellen."

"Afternoon, Mr. Adams," she said.

Mr. Adams gave a look at Davis and asked Mae, "Does your mama know you're out here?"

"Yes, sir. I was just inside, and she saw me."

Mr. Adams tapped his foot on the pavement. "You might want to give the customers a chance to sit for a spell, all right?" He turned, the automatic doors opened, and Mr. Adams disappeared.

Mae looked around. "You see any customers?"

"I think I'm the problem," Davis said, finishing off a third cookie. "You shouldn't be sitting out here with me."

"What's wrong with you?" Mae asked.

Davis tilted his head and looked at Mae over his sunglasses.

"Oh. That." Mae remembered Davis was the talk of the town when he'd gotten dumped by the Braves on account of he was a drug addict with anger management issues.

"You don't seem so bad," Mae said.

"That's because you don't know me." Davis wiped the corners of his mouth with his thumb. He looked at his watch. "I've killed enough time out here. I better get to Smith's."

Davis stood and brushed crumbs from his pressed shirt. He removed his cap and turned to see his reflection in the store's window. He ran his fingers through his thick black hair.

"You looking to buy some hardware?" Mae asked.

Davis smirked. "No. I'm looking for a job."

"A job? You're going from playing baseball to selling hammers?"

He nodded.

Things were definitely headed south since getting released from the Braves. Davis's only friend in town was an eleven-year-old girl, and he was looking for employment in a place where they answered the phone, "Smith's Hardware, where there's a bolt for every nut."

"Can I ask you something that's been bugging me?" Mae asked.

"Make it quick. My interview's in five minutes."

"You remember that championship game? The Tigers were losing and you were pitching?"

"I vaguely remember it," Davis said. He grinned real big.

"You hit the batter—"

"He leaned in," Davis interjected.

"Yeah, yeah, I know. He steals second and then gets to third on a wild pitch. The coach is gonna take you out, but you convince him to let you stay. It coulda cost Jessup the state title. What'd you say to him to make him change his mind?"

Davis stood still and quiet. It was as if he was standing on the mound like he did that day, glove held to his mouth to hide his words. "I said, 'Let me finish the job.'"

Mae nodded, satisfied she'd finally discovered what was said in that private conversation. She wanted to know more, but he'd already moved down the sidewalk.

Davis stopped in front of Smith's Hardware Store. It looked like he was considering whether or not he should go in. Then he turned and kept on walking down Main Street.

CHAPTER NINE

At cookie number five, Mae decided she'd better stop, even though chances were good the last few would melt before she got them home to her daddy and Shelby. Jimmy Mac must have smelled them from his house, because he rode up and parked his bike next to hers.

"I see you got your tire fixed," Mae said.

He sat beside her. "Took it to the gas station, and they fixed it right up."

"Cookie?" She set the white box in his lap.

"You bet!" He reached in and took one with each hand.

"Double-fisting it today, huh?" she said.

"I ain't had no breakfast."

Mae's eyebrows knitted together. Jimmy Mac's mama babied him something terrible. She would no more let him leave the house with an empty stomach than him wearing shorts and flip-flops. She was scared a tick might latch on and give him Lyme disease.

"No breakfast?"

He'd already stuffed one cookie into his mouth and was starting on another. "Mama's not feeling good. I left before she woke up."

Mae's eyes widened. *That's it!* she thought. Jimmy Mac's mama was sick. That's why he was needing prayer.

Eating seemed to loosen him up. "Have another one," she said. "Your mama got a cold?"

Jimmy Mac took another cookie. "Not exactly."

"Stomach bug?"

"Nah."

"Strep throat?"

"She's just tired," he said.

It didn't sound right to Mae. Jimmy Mac's mama worked in the school cafeteria, and she moved quicker than a jackrabbit hopping across hot asphalt. Mrs. Twila served up sloppy joes and tater tots to four hundred starved kids every day, and she never looked tired. Plus, it was summer. What was there to be tired about?

"Maybe she's just missing your daddy," Mae suggested.

"Whatcha want to do today?" Jimmy Mac asked.

Mae looked in the box. The cookies were gone, and the vault was shut tight. Jimmy Mac wasn't going to say any more about his mama, so she might as well move on.

"Wanna help me figure something out?" she asked.

"Sure. I ain't got nothing else to do. What is it?"

"I need to find a way to get Miss Fannie to bid on The Donut Hole so she can turn it into her own bakeshop."

Jimmy Mac's mouth hung open as he turned toward her. "Where'd you get an idea like that?"

Mae explained about Miss Fannie getting her hours cut at the grocery store and the possibility of her losing her home.

"Having a building don't mean you can start baking cookies to pay your rent," he said.

"But the place already has a kitchen, chairs, and tables." Mae stuck out a finger as she said each thing. "The cash register is even still there."

"What's she supposed to use to bid when she ain't got no money?" he asked.

Mae told Jimmy Mac about the sign saying "dirt cheap." Even Miss Fannie could come up with that.

"Okay, so all you have to do is get Miss Fannie to make a bid," he said, standing. "Let's go talk her into it." He stood and pushed his pants legs down.

"Hold your horses," Mae said, motioning with her hand for him to sit back down. "There's one problem I haven't mentioned."

"Lay it on me," he said.

Mae rested her head on the back of the bench and crossed her arms. "She might have some competition."

"Another bidder?"

Mae twisted her lips.

"Someone with a lot more dirt?"

Mae nodded. "Your girlfriend's mama."

Jimmy Mac shook his head and muttered, "Savanna's not my girlfriend."

Mae and Jimmy Mac sat side-by-side, neither one speaking, both contemplating how to better Miss Fannie's odds of winning the bid and ending her money troubles once and for all.

The preacher's prayer for Miss Fannie entered Mae's head, tempting her to believe a happy ending could come even when things didn't look so good. She wanted to believe—she did. It's just, the need to protect her heart from disappointment was as strong as the hope that something good could happen.

"I got it!" Jimmy Mac shot up.

"What?" Mae asked, straightening up too.

"What if—" Jimmy Mac started.

"Yes?

"We made it so Miss Fannie was the only bidder?"

"Go on," Mae said, lifting an eyebrow.

"What if The Donut Hole was no longer attractive to Mrs. Weatherall?" Jimmy Mac grinned as wide as the Chattahoochee River.

Mae noticed a gleam in his eye she'd never seen before. She liked it. "I'm listening."

They spent the better part of the afternoon discussing various pests that could move into The Donut Hole and make a certain prospective buyer rethink selling her peach cobblers there. Snakes were definitely out of the question. Even Mae was afraid of those. Rats were a no-go too. They gave both Jimmy Mac and Mae the willies. Spiders were a possibility—if Mae would agree to handle them solo. Jimmy Mac's mama had already scared the bejeebies out of him, telling him about black widows and brown recluses.

Then they came up with the perfect vermin. Frogs. Both of them were comfortable touching them—what was a wart or two for a good cause?

————

Mae and Jimmy Mac spent the rest of the afternoon hunting for frogs along the banks of the Hooch. They watched for movement under the trees and listened for the low ru-u-um sound of bullfrogs.

Within an hour, Mae had already caught ten. Maybe God was answering the preacher's prayer for Miss Fannie. Mae couldn't stop smiling, confident their plan to scare Mrs. Weatherall out of bidding would work.

Frog-catching didn't come as easily to Jimmy Mac. After the fourth frog slipped out of his hands, he resorted to searching for beetles and worms instead. The frogs would need to eat while hiding out in the old donut shop.

They headed to The Donut Hole with seventeen frogs in Mae's backpack and a water bottle full of frog food.

"How are we gonna get them inside?" Jimmy Mac asked.

Mae stopped pedaling and coasted to the four-way stop sign. "I haven't planned that out yet," she said, her backpack jumping behind her.

"Hey, one's getting away!" Jimmy Mac parked his bike and took off across the road. He grabbed the frog that had hopped out of Mae's backpack, rolled it up in his shirt, and carried it back to her. Jimmy Mac gave her a funny look.

"What?" she asked, smiling a show-your-teeth kind of smile.

He grinned big. "You look different."

"You don't look so hot yourself," she said.

"No. I mean—you look . . . happy."

Mae wasn't just happy. She was excited. There was a real chance something good was about to happen. Maybe things improving for Miss Fannie was just a start. Next, Mae would take care of Shelby while her parents went out. She'd do a good job this time and finally be forgiven for her worst sin.

"I'd be happier if you stopped yapping and started pedaling," Mae said, taking off. Mae's heart was light, and she was more determined than ever. "All we need is a cracked window."

"Huh?" Jimmy Mac asked, trying to keep up.

"If there's even a slit of an opening, we can drop the frogs through."

They turned onto Main Street and passed the Piggly Wiggly. They parked their bikes in the rusty bike racks catty-corner to The Donut Hole.

Mae hung back, struggling to get her backpack off without losing another frog. When Jimmy Mac reached the door, he read the orange sign. He looked back at her with a lost expression.

Mae pulled one strap off her shoulder. "What's wrong?" she shouted.

"When did the bids have to be in?" he yelled back.

Finally free of her backpack, Mae race-walked to the door. "The auction is July 17th," Mae said. "I remember because it's exactly one week before my parents' anniversary." She set the backpack full of frogs on the ground.

"Look," Jimmy Mac said, pointing at the sign. In big, bold letters over the "dirt cheap" part was the word "Sold."

Mae's heart dropped on the hard sidewalk. Her jaw lowered, but no words came out.

"We're too late, Mae. It's already sold."

"I know!" Her chin trembled. "I can read."

"Don't get all hot. It's just a dumb old building."

"You don't know nothing." Tears welled in her eyes. Mae figured Mrs. Weatherall must've beaten them to it and made an offer on the place. She and Savanna were probably already making enough peach cobblers to put Miss Fannie in money troubles forever.

Why did people who already had enough get more, and those who had nothing get even less? Mae should've known better than to count on that prayer. Letting her hopes rise up just meant disappointment was around the corner.

Mae grabbed the sign and tore it off the door with one quick rip. "Miss Fannie never did anything to hurt anybody!" She turned her backpack over and shook it. Frogs spilled out and shot every which way. Mae threw the empty backpack against the building. "It ain't fair!" She ran toward her bike.

"Wait up!" Jimmy Mac called after her.

Mae yanked her bicycle from the bike stand. "Stupid preacher!"

Jimmy Mac got to her as she was about to take off. He reached for her handlebars and held them steady. "Okay, Miss Fannie's not getting her bakery, but it's not the end of the world."

"Stupid prayer! All it does is get your hopes up," she said. "Nothing's ever gonna change."

"What are you talking about?" Jimmy Mac asked.

"I'm talking about the dang drive-thru!" She jerked her bike from his grasp. "Praying don't help nobody!"

"You've been to the drive-thru?"

"Yeah, and you might as well stop hoping, 'cause all the praying in the world won't do you no good either." Mae put a foot on her pedal.

"Wait." Jimmy Mac's face twisted like he was trying to figure things out. "Did you—"

"You're wasting your time, Jimmy Mac."

He clenched his teeth.

"Your mama ain't gonna stop being tired, or sad, or whatever's wrong with her." Mae's heart pounded. "You might as well get used to it. She's as good as gone."

Jimmy Mac got in Mae's face. "You take that back, Mae Ellen Moore."

"Make me!" she yelled.

A madness took over Jimmy Mac like a dark sky before a storm. He grabbed ahold of her shoulders and pushed harder than he'd pushed anything before. Mae's leg tangled up in the pedal, and she lost her balance. She fell on the pavement, her bike falling on top of her.

Jimmy Mac stood over her and shouted, "You've had hate in your heart for Savanna Weatherall and Bubba Duncan— heck, half the town! Now you're shouting hate at me?"

Mae lay there. She'd never seen him so angry before.

"What's hate gotten you? I feel sorry for you, Mae."

Mae clenched her jaw. She climbed out from under her bike and stood it up. She got on the seat, but Jimmy Mac stood between Mae and her escape. She gave him a laser-like stare, and Jimmy Mac knew she wouldn't think twice about running him over. He stepped to the side, and she pedaled fast down the street.

CHAPTER TEN

Mae wiped her eyes with the crook of her arm, and the bike swerved. She put both hands on the handlebars to steady it, arriving at the Hooch in record time. Her bike was still rolling as Mae hopped off and started down the embankment. She ran, dodging trees until a root sticking up grabbed her foot. She fell forward and tumbled the rest of the way, not stopping until the ground leveled out at the river's edge.

Her knee and elbow took the brunt of the fall. Both were scraped and bloody, but she didn't care. Mae yanked off her sneakers and flung them behind her. Next, her socks. She picked up a huge rock, lifted it over her head, and hurled it into the river.

She didn't have the patience for slippery stones today, so she waded through shin-deep water until she reached the middle of the river and her favorite thinking spot. The rock was smooth on top and big enough to keep most of her out of the water.

Each time she wiped her eyes, fresh tears escaped. Jimmy Mac's words played over and over in her head, putting an ache in her heart each time. She hated this feeling. It usually only came when she worried about Shelby. If her sister had a seizure or a breathing emergency, Shelby would end up in the ambulance. There was nothing Mae could do to stop it from happening. That's how she felt now—hurt. Helpless. Hopeless.

And now there was nothing to stop the hurt from what Jimmy Mac had said. *I feel sorry for you, Mae.*

Then she remembered how to stop it. *Who needs Jimmy Mac anyway?* she thought. *He can't play sports worth spit.*

"I HATE JIMMY MAC HARRIS!" She shouted so loud birds fluttered out of the trees above her.

Mae caught her reflection in the water. Her forehead was crinkled, her nostrils flared, and her fists balled up. She almost didn't recognize the person looking back at her. Mae kicked her foot, and ripples ran through her face in the water.

She didn't need anybody feeling sorry for her. Truth be told, Mae felt sorry for herself sometimes. And then the feeling turned into something worse. *Why do I have to have a sister who—*Mae put her head in her hands, her elbows propped up on her knees. *How could I be mad at Shelby? I'm a terrible sister,* she thought.

The water splashed beside her, and she turned around.

"Have you cooled off yet?" Jimmy Mac asked. He stood along the shoreline with the bottle of crickets in one hand and Mae's backpack in the other.

Mae turned her back to him so that he wouldn't see her dab her eyes with her shirt sleeve. She wiped her nose with the back of her hand.

She faced him. "*Me* cool off? You were the one doing the pushing."

"Sorry. I don't know what got into me," he said. He hung his head and shook it.

Mae's feet dangled in the river. "It might've been something I said."

"I don't remember." Jimmy Mac turned the bottle upside down and let the beetles and worms escape.

"I didn't mean what I said about your mama," Mae said.

"I know. And I didn't mean what I said."

"The part about me hating everybody or you feeling sorry for me?" Mae asked.

Jimmy Mac looked stuck. "Both. But maybe you could work on not wanting to punch Bubba Duncan or show up Savanna Weatherall all the time."

Mae shrugged her shoulders. "I'm not sure I can." She stood and waded back across the water.

Jimmy Mac held up Mae's shoes. "Could you at least try?"

She reached for her sneakers, but he yanked them back.

"Okay, I'll try." She snatched them out of his hand. Mae sat on the ground and put her socks and shoes on.

"How'd you know about my prayer?" he asked.

"Lucky guess?"

He shook his head.

"Okay. I saw you with the preacher. I hid in the woods and watched you," she confessed.

"You spied on me?"

"I think we're even," she said, reminding him of the time he had watched her almost save—or almost kill, depending on which version you believed—Bubba Duncan.

"They're getting a divorce, my mama and daddy." Jimmy Mac picked up another rock and threw it in the river. "Some days Mama won't get out of bed."

Mae tossed a rock in too. "Why didn't you tell me?"

"I don't know. I guess I was embarrassed." He walked to the tree stump and sat down. "I went to the church to pray for Mama. Ask how I could help her."

Mae leaned against a tree. Now her heart hurt for Jimmy Mac.

"You said something about prayer only getting your hopes up. What'd ya mean?" he asked.

Mae explained how she'd asked the preacher to tell her about Jimmy Mac's prayer. And that the preacher had finagled a way to get her to pray for Miss Fannie. And how it was a complete waste of time because The Donut Hole had probably already been sold by then.

They sat quietly for a while, each taking turns tossing rocks.

"I spent all my prayers on Shelby," Mae said. "I ain't got none left."

Jimmy Mac looked puzzled. "Praying ain't like wishing on some star. There's not a maximum number of prayers that you can say." Jimmy Mac was out of rocks he could lift, so he snapped a twig and threw both parts in. "Most likely, my mama's still gonna be in her pajamas when I get home, but it don't mean I'm gonna stop praying for things to change."

Mae thought about that. "I don't know, Jimmy Mac. Sometimes it seems like I ain't got no say in anything. Like things are gonna happen, no matter what I do or don't do."

He wiped the sweat off his forehead with his shirt sleeve and stood. "Life's complicated, Mae. All I know is talking to the preacher makes me feel better. And praying gives me hope—not because I'm going to get everything I ask for, but because God's listening."

Mae bent down and splashed water on her knee and elbow, both stained with blood.

"Gosh, Mae. I'm sorry! I didn't mean to push you so hard."

"I guess you don't know your own strength." She blew on her elbow scrapes to stop the sting. "I'll think twice before making you mad."

Mae grinned to herself. Jimmy Mac's confidence needed a little boosting, so if he thought he was strong enough to cause her injuries, she'd let him think it. She sort of owed him.

"I'd better get back. I wanna check on Mama," he said. "See you tomorrow?"

"'Course." Mae watched as he climbed the hill to his bike.

She cleared a spot under a huge tree and sat listening to the water as it rushed over the river rocks. It was so simple here—her and the Hooch—and she wished she could stay forever.

Mae wondered how long Jimmy Mac had held the secret of his parents' divorce inside. How long had he ached and not told anybody? Each time Mae's secret tried to climb out, it stomped on her heart as she tried to hold it down. What would it feel like to finally set it free?

After almost an hour, she started up the embankment to head home. But first, she needed to make a stop.

———

As Mae rode down the hill, she saw the preacher under his usual shade tree. There was something comforting about his predictability.

She pedaled along the church's driveway, then parked her bike. As she got closer, she saw him slouched in the chair, with his feet propped up on the cooler. He wore a large tan hat like a kid might wear when pretending to go on a safari. The hat was pulled way down, covering his eyes. She heard a low roar of a snore.

She didn't want to startle him, so she cleared her throat. Nothing. She looked around for something to tap him with and picked up a stick. She patted once gently on his arm. Eyes still closed, he swatted at the spot she touched.

Mae covered her giggle with her hand, and as she was about to tap him again—harder this time—bird poop drizzled on his hat. She looked in the tree above the preacher. A brown bird shook his tail feathers, and another dime-sized whitish glob splattered his hat.

"Shoo," she said in a loud whisper, waving the stick at the bird.

The preacher woke and pushed back his hat, avoiding the bird's droppings. "Well, hello, Mae Ellen. I was just—" he sat up in his brown woven lawn chair. "Well, I could say I was praying, but the truth is I was napping."

Mae looked at the preacher, then the bird poop, then the preacher again. "Uh-huh."

"Can I help you with something?" he asked. "Are you here for prayer?"

She tried to act like there was nothing disgusting on the top of his hat, but she couldn't un-scrunch her face.

"Is something the matter?" he asked.

"There's—you've got—" Mae wasn't sure if "poop" was the kind of word you could say in front of a preacher. "A bird did number two on your head."

"What?" The preacher removed his hat. "Doggone it. This is my favorite hat too," he said, shaking his head. He took a deep breath. "Well, God made all the creatures, even that one." He looked in the tree and gave the bird the stink eye. "He's probably in cahoots with Miss Wanda. She's been hoping I'd lose this thing."

The preacher set the hat on the ground, unfolded the lawn chair leaning against a tree, and placed it across from his.

Mae took a seat, not sure what to say next. Why did she have to listen to that tiny voice in her head suggesting she come?

"So what's the latest on Miss Fannie?" he asked. "Did you want to say another prayer for her?"

"It'd take more than prayer." Mae smoothed the dirt with her foot. "It'd take a miracle to fix Miss Fannie's money troubles."

He leaned forward and rested his elbows on his thighs. "How's that?"

"We're too late."

Mae explained about The Donut Hole going up for auction and how it would have been the perfect place for Miss Fannie to open up her own bakery. She told the preacher how she and Jimmy Mac found out the place was sold, and Miss Fannie's chance at a better life was gone.

Mae left out the parts where they had schemed to fill The Donut Hole with frogs and how Jimmy Mac had said she had hate in her heart. She especially left out the part where she told Jimmy Mac he was wasting his time on prayer.

"That's too bad," the preacher said. "How'd Miss Fannie take the news?"

Mae thought about it. She was definitely more disappointed about the whole thing than Miss Fannie was. Or might have been.

"She doesn't know," Mae said. "I just wanted something good to happen to somebody in this town, and Miss Fannie deserves some goodness more than anybody."

"You're a good friend, Mae Ellen." He leaned back in his chair and crossed his legs.

Mae considered correcting the preacher, but he'd discover soon enough what a horrible person she was.

"Can I ask you something?"

"Ask away." The preacher swatted at a mosquito buzzing around his ankle.

"Do you think God gives you what you ask for?"

He scratched his head. "That's a good question, Mae Ellen. Sometimes God answers our prayers with a yes. And sometimes with a no." The crease in his forehead relaxed. "Often He answers in ways we never expected."

"It's just—I've been praying for Shelby for as long as I could talk, and she ain't no better. Sometimes she's even *worse*."

The preacher started to say something, then stopped. "God works in mysterious ways."

Mae gave him a look like she wasn't satisfied with the answer.

"I can't explain why God does what He does." He rubbed his hand over the light gray stubble on his chin. "Or why sometimes bad things happen to good folks."

"Or why good things happen to bad people?" Mae asked.

"'For all have sinned,' Mae Ellen."

"Some more than others," she said, thinking of Savanna and Bubba.

Then she remembered all the hating she'd been doing and the mean words she'd yelled at Jimmy Mac just a couple of hours ago. She hung her head. She was ashamed that sometimes she was even mad at Shelby. Mad at all the attention she got from their parents. Mad they never seemed to have enough money because of her medical bills. Mad because people stared at them wherever they went.

And the worst sin—she sometimes wondered what it would be like if Shelby had never been born.

Mae squeezed her eyes tight. A tear fell on her knee, and she quickly wiped it away.

The preacher smiled. "'Faith, hope, and love.'"

"Love?"

Preacher Floyd nodded. "And the greatest of these is love.'"

Mae did love her sister. How could she also be mad at her? Mae's feelings were all tangled up. *Love.* More than anything, she wanted to prove she loved Shelby the way she was.

The preacher reached into his cooler and took out two bottled waters. He handed her one, and they both drank without saying a word. Every now and again birds whistled, and the preacher looked up to see if he might get poop-bombed.

"I don't know everything, Mae Ellen, but I'm certain of God's love for us, both in times of need and times of plenty. He loves each one of us, no matter our sins."

Even if somebody has horrible thoughts about her own sister? Mae wasn't sure if that sin was included.

"And He wants us to do the same," the preacher added, snapping Mae out of her thinking.

"Come again?"

"God wants us to love each other too."

"Oh," Mae said, remembering she'd told Jimmy Mac she'd try to stop hating Bubba and Savanna. "I was afraid you might say something like that."

Preacher Floyd chuckled. "Some folks are harder to love than others."

"You don't know the half of it." Mae's heart was quiet. Jimmy Mac was right—talking to the preacher did make her feel better, even if he didn't have all the answers. Or if some of the answers were the kind you didn't like.

Her water bottle was empty, and she set it on the ground. "Thank you."

"Any time."

Mae stood. As she walked toward her bike, the preacher asked, "Would you like to pray before you leave?"

She shrugged her shoulders. "I don't know what to say."

"Tell you what. I'll start, and you can jump in if you feel like it," he suggested.

The preacher prayed for Miss Fannie and for a blessing to come her way. Then he prayed for Mae's family, for each of them to have the courage required to handle any challenge they might face. When he hesitated a minute before saying "Amen," Mae jumped in and asked God to help Mrs. Twila get out of her pajamas and fuss over Jimmy Mac like she used to.

CHAPTER ELEVEN

Mae woke to the smell of bacon and cinnamon toast—her mama's specialty. Her daddy usually had breakfast duty, but Mae's mama didn't have to work today.

Shelby had already eaten and was watching the rebroadcast of last night's baseball game. "How'd we do?" Mae asked. The crowd roared when a player doubled and two Braves scored. Shelby slapped her palm on the arm of her wheelchair. Mae bent down and tied one of Shelby's shoes. "Tell me the score when I get back, okay?"

Mae went into the kitchen and sat at the table. Her daddy walked in, scratching sleep from his eyes. "I guess I overslept. Why didn't anybody wake me?" he asked.

"Happy anniversary!" Mae's mom said in a sing-song voice. "I thought I'd let you sleep in."

"But it's tomorrow," he said, looking over her shoulder at the bacon sizzling.

"Okay, I'm a day early. But I have to go in at six tomorrow, and I won't be able to make breakfast. Unless y'all want to get up with the roosters."

"No thank you, ma'am," Mae and her daddy said together. They looked at each other and laughed.

Mae's mama set down plates with strips of bacon and two pieces of cinnamon toast on each of them. "Eat up," she said.

Mae didn't hesitate. She'd need her strength today. She had anniversary plans of her own. It was a two-parter. Part 1: The anniversary cake. Miss Fannie would have the cake ready today, and Mae would ride to the grocery store to pick it up. Her only problem was carrying it home. But she had a plan. And it involved Bubba Duncan. Part 2: The special dinner. Mae would buy a gift card to Ralph's on the River, a fancy restaurant overlooking the Chattahoochee River. Her family had never been there, but every time they saw a commercial, their mouths watered. Golden-fried hush puppies and tender catfish served with your choice of three sides. It looked so good that it made you want to lick the TV. Well, that's what her daddy always said when the commercial came on. This part came with a challenge, too—getting her parents to agree to let her take care of Shelby for the evening. She needed to start laying the groundwork for that now.

"How long you and Daddy been married?" Mae already knew the answer, but she didn't want either of them to know she'd been cooking up a plan.

"Fourteen years," her mama answered.

"Yep. If I hadn't met your mama at the Valentine's dance, she'd be married to Sam Meredith right now."

Mae's mama crossed her arms and pursed her lips, then smiled.

Mae took a spoonful of sugar from the bowl and started to sprinkle it over her toast. "Whoa, girl," her daddy said.

She dumped most of the sugar back in the bowl but sprinkled the bit left on the spoon onto her toast. "What's ole Sam doing these days?" Mae asked.

Her daddy took a bite of bacon and pointed the rest of the strip at her. "He put all he had into some investment and quadrupled his money, then moved to Atlanta a millionaire."

Mae sighed.

"I doubled my money once." Her daddy took a sip of milk, and Mae wondered why she'd never heard this story. "Yep, folded over two dollars and stuck 'em back in my pocket."

Mae's mama laughed, spewing coffee. Mae shook her head, but she loved hearing her mama laugh. She wished she heard it more often.

"A special anniversary dinner sure would be nice." Mae kept her head low but watched to see if her hint took. "Just the two of you."

"I've got it all planned," her mama said. "The four of us will feast on chicken fried steak, mashed potatoes, and gravy prepared by Chef Leigh Ann."

It sounded fancier than her daddy's usual mac and cheese from a box with sliced hot dogs, but Ralph's on the River was way better. Mae smiled big, thinking about what her parents would say when she handed them the gift card. But first she had to get to the Piggly Wiggly to buy it.

After breakfast, Mae snuck into her parents' bedroom. She'd never called a boy before, and she shivered, thinking her first would be Bubba Duncan.

She took the school directory out of her stack of report cards and best B+ papers her mama had saved on the nightstand. She flipped the pages until she came to Bubba Duncan's family. Mae sat on the edge of the bed and practiced what she'd say.

She punched the buttons but hung up real fast before anyone had a chance to say hello. *My butter's done slipped off my cornbread,* she thought. She couldn't believe she was actually going to ask Bubba for help.

Mae watched the time change on her parents' clock beside their bed—9:15, 16, 17. But it wasn't like Bubba was doing her a favor—he owed her. He'd lost the bet after all.

She was stalling. It was best to get it over with. She punched the numbers again and heard a ring. Then another. Mae tapped her foot on the floor.

"Hello?" said a boy's voice.

"Look, you said if you didn't cross the river, you'd hitch your wagon to your bike and ride me around town. You lost fair and square. I don't know why I even agreed to that, but I need your wagon today. You'll carry me in it while I hold my parents' anniversary cake. So meet me at the Piggly Wiggly in thirty minutes. Get my cake, cancel your debt. Okay?" Mae was out of breath, saying the whole thing as if it were one long sentence.

"Who is this?" the voice asked.

Are you for-realin' me? Mae thought. "It's me!" she shouted. Then she whispered this time so that her parents wouldn't hear her, "It's Mae, Bubba."

"Oh. Hey, Mae. It's Beecher. Bubba ain't here," Bubba's cousin said.

Mae fell back on the bed, exasperated, with the phone still on her ear. "Where is he?"

"Don't know. He's been gone a couple of hours. Got up early this morning. Hang on a sec."

Mae heard a door slam and then silence.

She cupped her hand around her mouth and the phone and hollered, "Beecher?"

Nothing.

Then another door slam.

"His bike's still here, so he didn't go far. I'll tell him you called," Beecher said.

"You tell him to meet me at the Wiggly parking lot with his wagon. I mean it, Beecher. A bet's a bet."

"I was a witness to it, Mae. I promise I'll tell him."

Mae hung up the phone. She hated being in a position of needing something from somebody. Especially if that some-body was Bubba. But she couldn't walk the cake home or balance it on her handlebars. Bubba was all she had.

She looked in the hall to be sure no one saw her coming out of her parents' room. The coast was clear, so she walked through the kitchen and headed for the door.

"Where you going?" her mama asked.

"Uh, you know. Here and there," Mae answered. She definitely sounded like she was up to something.

Her mama wrinkled her forehead and said, "I'm going to need you to be a bit more specific."

"I'm gonna meet Jimmy Mac at the grocery store. Get a free cookie, and then head to the Hooch." Mae didn't want to lie to her parents, but this was for a good cause.

"I'm thinking about making French bread pizza for lunch. I can't guarantee your daddy won't eat all of it."

Mae smiled big. "I'll be back by noon." She ran out the front door. Mae loved her mama's French bread pizza. She smothered it with cheese and topped it with big pepperoni slices. It was one thing if Bubba didn't show with the wagon so that she could transport the cake. But if he made her late for French bread pizza, he was dead meat.

———

Mae arrived at the Piggly Wiggly earlier than usual. She needed to get the cake home before the outside temperature cranked high enough to melt the icing.

She walked through the doors and headed straight for the gift card carousel. It had every card imaginable. There were cards to download music to your cell phone—if you actually had a cell phone.

There were gift cards for clothes, bedding, home fix-its, gasoline, baby clothes, sporting goods, movie tickets, and video games. It was like there was an entire mall right inside the Piggly Wiggly. She moved to the other side of the carousel and found the restaurant gift cards. There were tons to choose from—fast food, fancy food, food in between. Finally, she found a fifty-dollar Ralph's on the River card. It was yellow and had a huge fish on it. Its mouth was wide open, and a skinny man—most likely, Ralph—was throwing a hush puppy in it.

Mae walked down the center aisle and straight to the bakery. She saw Earlene standing behind the counter. Earlene usually filled in when Miss Fannie was out sick. She couldn't bake worth a flip, but she could load the sweets into the white boxes, tie a pretty bow, and make a sale. But where was Miss Fannie? And more importantly, where was the anniversary cake?

"Hey, Earlene," Mae said. "Miss Fannie here?"

"Hey, Mae Ellen," she said, adjusting her hairnet. "She took the day off." Earlene grabbed a brown wooden spoon, scooped a heap of icing out of a white tub, and licked it. "Buttercream," she said. "Fannie can tell the buttercream icing from the cream cheese just by looking, but I have to taste 'em to be sure."

Mae didn't have time for small talk, but she liked to point out the obvious. "It says 'buttercream' on the side of the tub," Mae said.

"Well, looky there," Earlene said, licking the back of the spoon. "Fannie said you might be coming in. She made your cake at her place. Said she wanted to do it up nice and didn't want the clock ticking to make her nervous. You know where she lives, right?"

Mae nodded. "Happy Acres Trailer Park. But I don't know which one's hers."

"Me neither. I'd walk by all of 'em and pick the one that smells like cookies," Earlene suggested.

Mae stood behind two customers in the check-out line. She looked above the doors at the huge pig-faced clock. It had been exactly thirty-five minutes since she'd talked to Beecher.

When it was her turn, she took out the crumpled bills and coins from her pocket and handed it all to the teenage cashier.

"Oooh, I love Ralph's," the girl said, swiping the card. "They have the best hush puppies."

"Uh-huh." Mae tapped her foot nervously. She glanced at the doors. Surely Bubba would be outside with his bike and wagon by now.

Mae thanked the cashier, slipped the gift card in her back pocket, and walked outside. No Bubba. She sat on the bench to wait. Ten minutes later, she was still there. Waiting. Fuming.

Mae walked around the corner in case he was standing in the side parking lot. He wasn't.

"Dang Bubba," she mumbled to herself as she went around front. "It was stupid to think I could trust him!" She kicked the bench hard and stubbed her big toe. Mae grabbed her shoe and hopped around on one foot until she smacked into Davis, who was trying to walk inside the store.

"You all right?" he asked.

Mae plopped on the bench. "No. I was waiting on somebody, but he's a no-show."

Davis turned to walk into the Wiggly.

"You working at the hardware store?" Mae asked. She removed her shoe to inspect the damage.

"No. I decided I wasn't cut out for that line of work."

"Oh. What are you cut out for?" Mae's mama always got on to her for asking nosy questions, but Mae couldn't help it. Some people were good at checkers. Mae was good at getting information.

Davis smiled. "I thought I'd try to get back in shape."

"In case the Braves take you back?"

"I'm not holding my breath." He stepped on the sensors, and the Wiggly doors parted. "And I'm not really advertising it either. I don't want to disappoint everybody again."

Mae nodded. She knew it was dangerous to get your hopes up too high.

"I'm getting a coffee and biscuit to go. Then I'm heading over to the high school weight room to work out." He pointed to her foot. "You need a bag of ice?" he asked.

"Nope, but I could use a favor."

CHAPTER TWELVE

Mae's bike slid around in the back of Davis's truck as they headed down Main Street. "Make it quick, okay? I ain't got all day to play taxi to you and your cake," Davis said.

"It'll be fast, I promise," she said. For a split-second Mae thought about finding Bubba's trailer and giving him a piece of her mind for not making good on their bet.

"I'm only doing this to get one of Miss Fannie's famous cookies," he said.

"Famous only at the Piggly Wiggly."

"What happened to her getting The Donut Hole?" he asked.

So he was listening that day on the bench, Mae thought. "Long story. It was a dumb dream." She looked out the window. "I had to let it go."

"I'm not sure how she would have managed under the pressure—owning her own bakery. It'd push her way outside of her comfort zone." He looked at Mae and gave her a sideways smile. "Still, her cookies are the best around," he added.

Davis pulled onto the dirt road that led to the trailer park, and they bounced along like they were riding the bumper boats at a summer carnival. The truck's tires kicked up a rock, hitting Davis's windshield. It sounded like a bullet and startled Mae as they rocked along the tree-lined road.

Davis thumped the steering wheel with his fingers to the song on the radio. He looked like the old Davis. Mae couldn't figure out how someone who had the opportunity of a lifetime could throw it all away. *Didn't he know he had something special?* she thought.

They finally came to a faded wooden sign tacked to a tree. It said, "Welcome to Happy Acres Trailer Park," with an arrow pointing the way. Mae watched out the window as they passed a bicycle, missing both tires, lying along the road. A little farther, she saw an old, rusted car stuck halfway in a ditch.

Through the trees, Mae spotted a burned-out trailer, its windows busted and roof missing. Kudzu grew out of every open crevice, and someone had spray-painted, "I'm melting" on one side.

Mae thought there was nothing "happy" about this place, and a better name for the trailer park might be "Gloomy Acres." She thought about the trailer park kids, like Bubba, riding the bus each day, seeing these same sights as they came and went. It would have given Mae the willies, but she wondered if they had gotten used to it like she'd gotten used to seeing the Burger Barn on the way to and from her house.

Only—you could get a banana cream milkshake and fried pickles at the Burger Barn. So probably not.

A small dog barked and nipped at the truck's tires as they came to the first trailer. "Which one's Miss Fannie's?" Davis asked.

Mae had hoped there'd only be a few trailers, but there were at least twenty, maybe thirty, all stuck back in the woods, like another world she didn't know existed. "Good question," she said.

"Dang, Mae. Were you planning on knocking on each door until you found hers?" Davis asked.

Mae was embarrassed. Her plan had been so well thought out. "No! My plan was to pick up the cake at the Piggly Wiggly. Only Miss Fannie wasn't there, so now we're here."

"One pass through the trailer park," Davis said. "Then we're out of here, cake or no cake."

Mae sighed loudly.

"We need to minimize the possibilities," Davis said.

"Good idea. Stick your nose out the window and holler if you smell something sweet," Mae suggested. They pushed the down buttons for the windows, stuck their heads out, and took a whiff. Then they jerked their heads back in.

"Whoa, that ain't nothing sweet," Mae said, holding her nose.

"Smells like a sewage line busted," Davis said. "Put 'em up."

They rolled up the windows and rode along slowly, examining each trailer that might belong to Miss Fannie. Two toddlers played outside while their mama watched from their trailer's steps. They wore only pull-ups and dug in the dirt with plastic shovels. Mae locked eyes with one of them as they passed, and the little girl waved. Mae lifted her hand to the window and smiled.

There was a trailer missing its front door and another with a washing machine in the yard.

Two "Miss Fannie" possibilities stood next to each other. They were simple, but nice. The grass was cut short, and curtains hung in the windows. Mae made a mental note for when they circled back and she began knocking on doors.

The next trailer wasn't broken down like some of the others, but it wasn't as nice as the Miss Fannie possibilities. Green vines snaked up the sides of the trailer and around the windows, and the once yellow siding on the front had faded to beige. It was a big one—a double-wide—and Mae giggled to her herself thinking it would be perfect for Bubba. *A double-wide for Double Wide.*

As they passed it, she saw two bikes lying on the ground and a wagon. It was old, but it was the SUV of wagons, with its sides tall enough to cart beach chairs and sandcastle building equipment, if you ever actually went to the beach. A wagon like . . .

"Stop!" Mae yelled.

Davis slammed on the brakes. Coffee sloshed out of his cup even though it had a top. He growled and grabbed a used napkin off the floor to wipe up the mess. "Do you see her?"

"No. I think that's where Bubba lives," she said, pointing to the trailer.

"Does Bubba have your cake?" Davis asked.

"Noooo. But that kid—" The bird that had pooped on the preacher's hat flashed in her mind. And how the preacher had said, "God made all the creatures, even that stinkin' bird," although she added the "stinkin'" part. Then she thought about what Jimmy Mac had said about her hating, and maybe Bubba was just a stinkin' kid creature. One she was supposed to love anyway.

Mae shook her head, wanting to get rid of the last part about loving Bubba.

The road split off in two directions ahead, and Davis looked at the clock on his dashboard.

"Let's go right," she said before he could say they had to head home.

"Nah, it doesn't go anywhere," Davis said.

Mae looked at him. "How do you know?"

"I just do," he snapped. "I'll drive down this last street, and then I'm taking you home."

They passed another row of trailers in silence. Mae secretly hoped none of them belonged to Miss Fannie. One looked dark and empty, except for a sofa in the yard with a cat stretched out on its torn cushions. A truck stacked high on cinder blocks, missing its tires and hood, sat in front of another.

The next one was definitely a possibility. The trailer needed a paint job, but it still looked inviting, with a wicker rocking chair sitting on a white porch. The front door opened, and two little kids walked out, each holding a cookie.

Mae and Davis looked at each other. "I say you start there," Davis said.

"What do I say if it isn't Miss Fannie's?" she asked.

"Ask for two cookies."

Mae got out of the truck. She hesitated and turned back to see Davis. He waved his hand at her like he was nudging her along.

She stepped onto the porch and noticed the curtains were cracked just enough to peek in. She inched up to the window, hoping to catch a glimpse of whoever was inside. Mae looked in, then stepped back and whipped her head around. She was shocked at what, make that *who*, she'd seen. She got close and looked in again. She couldn't believe it.

Mae folded her arms, walked down the porch steps, then back up. She reached to knock on the door, then put her hand down.

Davis tapped lightly on the horn, and Mae turned to stare at him, her hands on her hips. She took a deep breath and knocked on the trailer door.

The door swung open wide. "Mae Ellen! You're right on time. We've just put on the last rose," Miss Fannie said.

Mae walked past Miss Fannie straight into the kitchen. "What do you think you're doing to my parents' anniversary cake?"

Bubba put down the spatula and wiped his hands on his shirt. "*Your* parents' cake?" His ears turned bright red.

Miss Fannie followed behind her. "Simmer down, Mae Ellen. I'm teaching Bubba how to bake. He's like my, you know, one of them people who learns a trade by watching an expert."

Mae raised her eyebrows.

Miss Fannie changed the tip on her piping bag. "My apprentice."

"Miss Fannie's apprentice," Bubba whispered to himself.

"He's pretty good too. He was the one who dreamed up the recipe for the chocolate peanut butter cookies the other day. They weren't much to look at, but we can fix that."

Miss Fannie held the icing bag. "Bubba, you wanna squeeze the bottom of the pastry bag like this."

"Yes, ma'am," Bubba said.

He and Mae leaned in and watched Miss Fannie write on the cake. Mae noticed how Bubba studied Miss Fannie's technique. No wonder Beecher didn't know where his cousin was. It wasn't like Bubba would announce to the world he was decorating a cake.

"It's red velvet with a cream cheese frosting." Miss Fannie spun the cake around. "Whatcha think?"

Mae looked at the beautiful circular cake. It was tall—it had to be three, maybe even four, layers high underneath the thick icing. The cake was loaded with roses, all different shades of pink, with light green leaves. "Happy 14th Anniversary to the World's Nicest Couple!" was written in the center.

"It's beautiful." Mae looked at Bubba. "Did you—"

"Heavens, no," Miss Fannie interrupted. "He's practicing on the dummy cake." She pointed to a square cake on the counter.

It had lopsided globs that looked like flowers when Mae squinted her eyes, but they more closely resembled very lumpy marshmallows.

"He's coming along. Coming right along," Miss Fannie added.

Bubba grinned big. Then he looked at Mae and dropped his eyes to the floor.

"Good heavenly days!" Miss Fannie shouted. "How are you getting this cake home?"

Mae explained Davis Hampton was outside, and he'd take her and the cake home in his truck. Bubba asked if it was *the* Davis Hampton. Mae said it was, then warned to not go sounding like a fool and asking for his autograph because it was a touchy subject. Bubba nodded like he understood.

Miss Fannie boxed up the cake and handed it to Mae as if it was a newborn baby. "Bubba, you go on home now," Miss Fannie said. "We'll discuss flaky pie crusts tomorrow."

Bubba followed Mae out the door, and she stopped quick. Bubba smacked into her like a bulldozer, and Mae almost dropped the cake.

"Lawd, have mercy!" Miss Fannie hollered, raising her arms in the air.

"Sorry," Bubba said.

"You wouldn't happen to have a cookie I could give Davis, would ya?" Mae asked.

"I sure do," she said, going back into the kitchen. She wrapped three cookies in a paper towel and tied it with the same string she'd used to tie the cake box.

"Can I take 'em out to Davis?" Bubba asked.

"You promise not to make a scene?" Mae asked. "He's kinda sensitive."

"Promise."

"C'mon then."

They walked to the truck. Bubba even opened the door so that Mae could get in without having to balance the cake with just one hand. She slid onto the seat and held the cake on her lap. Bubba reached over her and handed Davis the cookies without saying a word.

"Bubba Duncan, Davis Hampton," Mae introduced.

"Hey," Bubba mumbled. He stared at Davis like he was meeting a celebrity for the first time. Most likely because he *was* meeting a celebrity for the first time.

Davis raised the cookies to his nose and took a whiff. "Triple Cs?"

"Huh?" Bubba asked.

"Chocolate-Chocolate Chip. Triple Cs," Davis explained.

It was like a rock had thunked Bubba in the head and jarred his brain. "Ohhhhh. Yeah. I get it," Bubba said, grinning big.

"That's what we called them when I was a kid," Davis said.

Mae bugged out her eyes, sending a message to Bubba he needed to move so that she could shut the door. He stepped away and closed it for her.

Davis turned the truck around, and Mae watched Bubba out her window. He waved his hand in the air like a super-fast windshield wiper during a downpour. Mae scrunched her nose and gave him a half wave. She'd seen a different side of Bubba, and she wasn't sure what to make of it.

Davis and Mae got back on the paved road. He unwrapped the cookies with his left hand and shoved one in his mouth. He saw Mae staring at him. "Whaaa?" he asked, his mouth full.

She shook her head. "Too bad you couldn't be hooked on Miss Fannie's cookies instead of drugs."

Davis swallowed hard. "It was prescription medication."

"You mean like the pink stuff you take when you have strep throat? They want you to think it tastes like strawberries, but it don't," Mae said, making a face like she'd eaten pie made of dirt and worms.

"Not amoxicillin, goof. It was pain medication."

"Oh."

"Only I wasn't addicted to that either," he said, staring straight ahead at the road.

"Then what was wrong with you?" Mae asked.

"It's a long story," he said.

"I got time."

So Davis told Mae how he threw it all away. He explained how he knew he was good—really, really good. But once he got to spring training, he saw he was one of many. The something special only he had back in Jessup was nothing compared to the other players who'd also gotten drafted by the Braves.

Mae turned sideways in the seat and listened. She wondered if he'd told his story to Preacher Floyd that day at Hopewell.

"I guess in order to compensate for feeling less than, I started talking big, acting big," Davis said, staring at the road ahead.

"Too big for your britches?" Mae asked.

"Yeah." Davis nodded. "One night I was pitching—doing pretty good too, I thought—and the coach said he was taking me out. We had words on the mound, and then I said more words in the dugout."

"Lost your temper?" Mae asked.

Davis nodded again. "I might've thrown a bat at him."

Mae slapped her forehead with her hand. "Good golly, Miss Molly," Mae said, sounding like her daddy.

"It was a long time before I got the chance to pitch again, and when I did, I was a bundle of nerves. I didn't think I was good enough anymore."

"You got scared?"

"Yep. The more scared I got, the worse I played. And the worse I played, the more scared I got." Davis turned to her and made a circle in the air with his finger. "It became a cycle I couldn't break."

"Then you hurt your back?" Mae asked.

"No. I got cut, so I made up the part about hurting my back and getting hooked on prescription drugs. It seemed like a better reason for getting kicked out of baseball and being sent home. Made me sound tougher." He paused. "I know it sounds messed up now."

Mae looked out her window and thought about Shelby and how she always rode to the river whenever the ambulance showed up. "I get scared sometimes."

"Everybody does." Davis turned his head toward her. "Fear seems to show up most when we put faith in the wrong things."

Mae raised an eyebrow. "You mean you should've trusted your pitching?"

Davis shook his head. "It's not so much about *what* you put your faith in, but *who*."

Mae's brain hurt like the time in fifth grade when the teacher was explaining how to find the volume of a prism.

"It's not like I got it all sorted out," Davis said. "I'm still working on it, and Preacher Floyd's helping me."

Mae sighed. "I figured you were praying for your back to get better."

Davis smiled. "I've been asking God for a second chance."

Mae pointed to her street. She thought about how the preacher had said your prayers sometimes get answered in ways you don't expect. "You're sort of like an answer to prayer."

"I hate to tell ya, but I ain't nobody's answer to prayer," he said, turning toward her house.

"But if you hadn't gotten released by the Braves, you wouldn't be in Jessup right now giving me and this cake a ride."

Davis chuckled. "I guess something good *can* come from something bad."

They pulled into her driveway. Mae opened her door and carefully slid out of the seat, holding the cake level. Davis took her bike out of the back of his truck and stood it up in her yard. "Tell your parents happy anniversary for me."

Mae nodded. "I hope you get it."

Davis looked confused.

"Your second chance," Mae said. She pushed the truck door shut with her hip and watched Davis back out of the driveway.

CHAPTER THIRTEEN

Mae took a deep breath. She'd accomplished Part 1 of the anniversary challenge—the cake. She'd managed to get it safely home with a little help from Davis. And absolutely no help from Bubba Duncan, thank you very much.

The picture of Bubba standing in Miss Fannie's kitchen, holding a spatula, crossed her mind. This was the perfect ammunition. The next time Bubba even thought about crossing Mae, she'd—

Mae thought about Jimmy Mac and how he wanted, maybe even needed, her to be nicer to folks. Maybe he had put up with her short fuse long enough. Being nicer to Bubba probably included not teasing him about baking cakes. She nodded to nobody, having settled it in her mind. Now on to Part 2 of the anniversary challenge.

Mae pressed the doorbell, and her mama opened the screen door.

"Special delivery," Mae announced.

"What do you have there?" her mama asked.

Mae set the box on the kitchen table. "Where's Daddy?"

"Out back. He and Shelby are on one of their nature walks." Her mama grabbed a hot pad, opened the oven, and took out the French bread pizzas. "What's in the box?" she asked.

Mae ran through the living room and yelled out the open window that looked into the backyard. "Daddy! Shelby! Come see the surprise!" Then she ran back to the kitchen. "Wait 'til you see it."

"Why wait? Let's open it now," Mae's mama suggested.

"No! It's for both of you."

Her mama huffed, pretending to be mad. She leaned against the kitchen counter. "What if I don't want to share?" she asked.

Mae hugged her. "Happy anniversary!"

Her mama squeezed her tight. She moved Mae's bangs out of her eyes with her fingers and looked at her face. They stood with arms linked until Mae's daddy wheeled Shelby into the kitchen.

"Where's the fire?" he asked.

"Mae's got a surprise for us."

Mae let go of her mama, bent down, and whispered in Shelby's ear, "It's an anniversary cake." She looked at her mama and said, "I know it's a day early, but you're off today, and I wanted you to see it."

"Let's cut the chitchat and open this baby," her daddy said. Her daddy and mama looked at Mae for permission. She nodded her head fast up and down. Her daddy untied the string and opened the box. Mae bounced on her tiptoes. She couldn't wait for them to see the cake.

Her parents looked inside the box, and her mama said, "Oh, Mae Ellen, it's beautiful!"

"Who knew you could bake?" her daddy said.

Mae giggled. She knew he was kidding, but it still cracked her up to think she hadn't baked and decorated the cake, but someday Bubba might.

Mae explained how she'd ordered the cake at the grocery store, but Miss Fannie had made it at her house. When she got to the part about Davis Hampton giving her a ride, her daddy asked, "*Our* Davis Hampton?" kind of like Bubba had.

Her mama said she didn't like Mae accepting rides from strangers, and her daddy replied, "Oh, Davis ain't a stranger." He reminded Leigh Ann that Mae and he had cheered for Davis at all those home games. Then he reminded her Davis was Mrs. Willene's son. They were practically neighbors— only the Hamptons lived in a nice subdivision on the other side of the Piggly Wiggly. He should have stopped there, but he added Davis had been home since getting released from the Braves on account of his drug problem.

"Drug problem?" Mae's mama shouted.

Mae wanted to tell them the truth about Davis, but she decided it was, as the preacher put it, confidential information.

"He's worked it out, Leigh Ann," her daddy said, getting plates out of the cupboard.

"That's the truth," Mae said. She opened the refrigerator and took out the milk. Then she got glasses and set them on the table.

"You do the honors," her daddy said, handing her mama the cake slicer. "And I'll take a big piece with lots of roses."

Mae's mama almost cut into the cake when she stopped and hollered for somebody to get her phone and take a picture first.

They sat at the table eating Miss Fannie's cake, and the only sounds were "mmmmm" and "ohhhhh." Her daddy dabbed icing on Shelby's tongue, and she blinked her eyes. "She wants more," Mae said, and her daddy did it again.

"That Fannie. She's outdone herself this time," her mama said, licking the back of her fork.

Mae ran to her bedroom and opened her desk drawer. She took out the card she'd been working on ever since her daddy mentioned the anniversary. She slipped the gift card out of her back pocket, tucked it into the envelope with the note, and licked the flap.

"Where'd you run off to?" her daddy asked as she walked back into the kitchen.

Mae handed the card to him. He opened it as her mama looked over his shoulder. They read what Mae had written on the inside:

There once was a pretty and nice girl named
   Leigh Ann
Who went to the Valentine's Dance with a foot-
   ball player named Sam.

Sam drove a fancy car, but he couldn't dance
And when he acted like a jerk, Gary saw his
    chance.
Now it's Gary, Leigh Ann, and their girls—
The best family in the whole wide world.

Mae's mama started to cry and looked away. She always said she was an ugly crier and hated looking all splotchy. She dabbed her tears with the back of her hand and turned around.

"Don't cry, Mama," Mae said.

"Oh, don't mind her. She's just crying over the convertible she could have had if she'd married Sam," Mae's daddy said.

Mae's mama swiped him on the arm with an oven mitt. "Hush. This is the sweetest card. And the cake—I can't believe you did all this. It's the best anniversary ever. Thank you, Mae Ellen."

"But wait! There's more!" Mae yelled, sounding like the voice on the commercials selling comfy butt cushions or super fast blenders. "It must've gotten stuck in the envelope."

Her daddy shook the envelope, and the gift card fell upside down on the table. Mae's parents cocked their heads and read it together, "Ralph's on the River."

"Fifty dollars worth of Ralph?" her daddy asked.

"You can get all the hush puppies you want!" Mae exclaimed.

"This is too much!" her mama said. "You must have spent every cent you had."

"It's not every day you get to celebrate being married for fourteen years," Mae said. "You can go to Ralph's on your anniversary tomorrow night while I watch Shelby." She turned to her sister, "It'll be a girls' night—just you and me, Shelbs."

Mae's parents looked at each other. The mood soured. "The four of us can go to Ralph's. It'll be a family affair," her daddy said.

"No, Daddy. This is meant for you and Mama—like a date night. I can take care of her. Let me." Mae watched her parents glance between themselves again.

"I don't think—" Mae's daddy started, but her mama put her hand on his shoulder.

"We'll talk it over and let you know tomorrow," she said.

"Who wants another piece of cake?" her daddy asked, holding the cake slicer in the air like a sword.

Mae's mama looked at the pizzas cooling on the stove. "Who wants pizza when you can have cake? We'll save those for supper."

———

Later that night Mae tiptoed past her parents' bedroom on the way to get a drink of water. She stopped to listen when she heard her mama say, "We can't keep her small forever. It's time we gave her some responsibility."

Then her daddy said, "But the last time—"

"That was two years ago, Gary," her mama said.

Mae leaned against the wall and closed her eyes. Her parents couldn't forget that day any more than she could.

The day she was supposed to be watching Shelby while her daddy drove to Burger Barn. The day she froze when Shelby had her seizure.

"I think she can do it," her mama said.

"She's not ready," her daddy said.

"Sometimes Mae Ellen gets lost, ignored—"

"I know," her daddy interrupted. "I worry about that too."

Mae was surprised her parents thought about, even worried about her. With all the time they spent taking care of Shelby, Mae figured there wasn't anything left for fretting over her. But there was, and they did.

Mae took a step, and the floorboard squeaked. She turned around and hurried back to bed, still thirsty.

She plopped her head on her pillow and stared at the ceiling. Mae wanted her parents to have something nice—a night out, just the two of them, like normal parents.

Maybe if she hadn't left Shelby alone that day to ride her new bike in the yard. Maybe if she'd stayed put when the ambulance came instead of racing to the river. If she had stuck around, they might think she could handle taking care of Shelby. But she was scared too. Scared of what might happen. And it'd be all her fault—again.

Mae thought about Davis and how he was afraid he couldn't pitch anymore. But it was being afraid that ruined it for him—not his pitching. *What was it Davis had said? Something about fear and faith?* Mae wanted to figure it out so that fear would stop chasing her. But some things—like bad things happening to good people—didn't make any sense. Jimmy Mac was right. Life was complicated.

CHAPTER FOURTEEN

When Mae went into the kitchen the next morning, her daddy and Shelby were eating breakfast. She sat down, put her elbows on the table, and held her chin in her hands.

"What's the matter with you?" Her daddy wiped Shelby's face. "Somebody let out all the air in your tires?" he asked.

"Just tired, I guess." Mae walked all mopey to the cabinet and got a glass. She sighed loudly as she took out the orange juice from the refrigerator. She took a sip, then slouched in her chair.

"Maybe this'll put some whiskers on your catfish. Your mama and I have decided you can watch Shelby."

Mae shot up. "You mean it?"

"Your mama gets off work at three. We'll get to Ralph's right when they open at five and leave as soon as we're done eatin'."

Mae stood and hugged her daddy's neck. She gently squeezed her sister's shoulder. "We'll be fine, won't we, Shelby?"

Shelby pushed the table's leg with her foot, making the cake box shake. Her daddy looked at his bowl of corn flakes. "Who wants cake for breakfast?" he asked.

———

Mae was downright giddy the whole day—feeling all grown up. Her daddy noticed it too. He said if she'd do the laundry and wash the dishes, she'd feel so mature her head wouldn't fit in the house. She told him she didn't want to grow up *that* fast.

When Mae announced she was going to the grocery store, her daddy told her to be back early. He wanted to go over things for watching Shelby. Mae was sure she already knew those things, like important phone numbers and how to feed Shelby her supper. As she walked out the door, her daddy shouted, "Oh, and tell Fannie her cake was awful, but all will be forgiven if she'll make us another one—one even bigger this time."

———

Mae waved to her mama as she walked into the store. She headed straight for the bakery.

"Morning, Miss Fannie," Mae hollered, stepping up to the glass counter.

"Morning, Mae Ellen. Sounds like we did good, girl. Your mama told me everybody liked the cake."

"Liked it? There's only a smidge left!"

Miss Fannie smiled bigger than a slice of cantaloupe. Usually she'd cover her smile, ashamed of her absent front teeth, but not today. She beamed.

Miss Fannie reached over the counter and handed Mae a cookie. Mae had considered taking it easy on the sugar given the cake and all, but she was partial to one of her daddy's sayings: "carpe diem." She was pretty sure it meant to seize the cookie.

Mae took her usual place on the bench outside when Jimmy Mac pulled up on his bike and joined her. She told him about Bubba ditching her and Davis coming to the rescue. Then she told him about seeing Bubba in Miss Fannie's trailer.

"Bubba Duncan? Learning to bake? Are you sure?"

Mae nodded. "I can't shake loose the picture of him standing there with a spatula in his hand." Mae smiled. "And Miss Fannie says he's good at it."

"Just when you think you got somebody figured out, they go and show you another side," Jimmy Mac said, shaking his head.

"Well, this side's burned into my brain."

Mae described the anniversary cake and told him her parents said she was old enough to watch Shelby while they went out for a fancy dinner. She said this would be like convincing the manager of the Burger Barn to let her run the milkshake machine for the summer, but all Jimmy Mac said was, "Is there any cake left?"

Mae laughed.

"No, I mean it. Is there?"

"Come over later, and you can lick the icing off the box," Mae said.

"I guess it's better than nothing."

Savanna and her mother walked by, the strong smell of perfume hovering like a cloud. Savanna sat beside Jimmy Mac. "I'll wait out here," she told her mother. Savanna swung her feet back and forth, her rhinestone flip-flops showing off her perfectly pedicured toes.

If she mentions her mama buying The Donut Hole, so help me I'll—Mae thought. She sighed loudly, remembering her promise to Jimmy Mac. She was supposed to try to be nicer to Savanna too. Even the thought of it was exhausting.

Mae glanced at Savanna's hands. "Nice nails," Mae said, trying really hard to sound genuine. This was new for her, being nice to people she didn't like.

Savanna stuck her hands out and spread her fingers apart. "Passion pink's my favorite color." She looked at Jimmy Mac and smiled. His face turned red as he squirmed on the bench. "Have you heard the news?" Savanna asked.

"You have a crush on Jimmy Mac?" Mae whispered low enough so that only he could hear. Jimmy Mac elbowed her, his face turning redder.

"What news?" he asked Savanna, but he was looking at Mae.

Mae held her breath. *Here it comes,* she thought.

"Mother's peach cobbler recipe won second place in *Living and Eating in the South* magazine."

"What?" Mae asked, leaning over Jimmy Mac to look at Savanna.

Savanna nodded. "She's in there buying up all the copies to send to relatives."

"That's something," Jimmy Mac said. "Isn't it, Mae?"

"Mm-hmm," Mae hummed.

"Pretty soon she'll be selling her peach cobbler all over the state," Savanna added.

Mae leaned back against the bench and crossed her arms. Mae's niceness was wearing off. Jimmy Mac gave her a simmer-down look.

Mrs. Weatherall stepped out of the Piggly Wiggly, her arms loaded with magazines. "They only had twelve copies," she said, dropping two. Jimmy Mac hopped up and gathered them. "This will never cover everyone," she said.

Jimmy Mac tried to restack the two magazines on top of the heap, but Mrs. Weatherall kept turning this way and that. Mae figured she was looking to see if anyone was walking up the sidewalk so that she could show off her winning recipe.

"Come on, Savanna. We'll hit the drug store, then the Pick 'N Pack on Elm Street," Mrs. Weatherall said.

"We've got to get movin' too, don't we, Jimmy Mac?" Mae said, standing.

"Huh?" he said.

"Yeah, remember you wanted a piece of Miss Fannie's cake?" Mae headed for her bike. She flipped the kickstand up with her foot. "Miss Fannie made the most dee-licious cake."

"Come with us, Jimmy Mac. We could use your help," Savanna said, marching after her mother.

Mae raised her eyebrows.

Jimmy Mac looked at Mae, then at Savanna. His shoulders slumped.

"Hurry up," Savanna called over her shoulder. "Once we're through, Mother will take us to get milkshakes."

Mae pedaled slowly, turning to see if Jimmy Mac had gotten some sense. But he was still standing there, his feet glued to the sidewalk.

She rode home, mean thoughts directed toward Jimmy Mac. Then Mae figured spending an afternoon with Savanna was punishment enough. She wondered what the Weatheralls would call The Donut Hole. Mae tossed around a few ideas, then settled on The Peach Pits. She laughed at the thought of it the rest of the way home.

———

The screen door slammed behind Mae when she arrived home, notifying her daddy she was back.

"Good, you're home," he said, walking into the kitchen.

Mae took out a glass and filled it with water, then emptied it in almost one swallow. "Where's Shelby?"

"She's taking a nap. Pull up a chair, and let's talk turkey."

They sat at the table. Her daddy took out a piece of notebook paper and turned it over so that she couldn't read it. "Okay. Pop quiz. What number do you call if there's an emergency?" he asked.

Mae smiled big. "4-1-1."

"No fooling around, Mae Ellen."

"9-1-1," she said, punching an imaginary phone in the air.

"What's your mama's cell number?" he asked.

"If I had my own cell phone, I could pull up Mama's picture, and it'd call her automatically." Her daddy frowned and squinted his eyes, so she quickly recited her mama's cell number. She followed it with her daddy's number.

"Okay, you pass." He turned the paper over. "The numbers are here too, including Ralph's. I've already made Shelby Grace's supper and put it in the fridge. Warm up the mac and cheese in the microwave for forty-five seconds and give her some yogurt. We'll stop on the way home and get you something."

"Cheeseburger and onion rings?" she asked.

"You got it." He leaned back in his chair and sighed real big.

Mae patted his hand. "She'll be fine, Daddy. I got this."

He smiled. "I know you do. It's just we've never left Shelby Grace with anyone. Either me or your mama has always been with her." He patted her hand back. "Maybe it's time to let someone else help."

Mae stood and taped the paper with the phone numbers on it onto the wall by the phone. "Ralph's tonight and the movies next week," she said.

"Hold your horses, girl. I've got something else I want to discuss."

Mae felt her nerves start to rattle.

"Fried catfish or fried shrimp?" he asked.

Mae tapped her chin. "I'd go with the shrimp."

"I'll bring you home some hushpuppies."

"You better!" she said.

CHAPTER FIFTEEN

Later that afternoon, Mae sat in the kitchen with Shelby when they heard their mama's high heels click in. She swirled in her yellow dress with the tiny embroidered blue and white flowers. "What do ya think?" her mama asked.

Mae whistled. The last time her mama had worn the dress was three years ago when she'd gone to Atlanta to see her friend get married.

The three Moore girls sat together at the kitchen table while Mae's daddy lingered in the bathroom, sprucing up. He'd been in the pantry twenty minutes earlier looking for a bandage after he'd nicked his chin shaving.

"Mae Ellen, are you ready?" her mama asked.

"For what?"

Her mama smiled. "We should've let you help out before tonight. You're more than capable." She combed Mae's bangs with her fingers. "I know it's not always easy. You might even feel a little forgotten at times."

Not so much anymore, she thought. Mae knew eaves-dropping on her parents' conversation the night before was wrong, but it made her feel better knowing they cared about her feelings.

"Ta-da!" Her daddy tap-danced into the kitchen—only it was more like stomp dancing. Shelby looked at the floor and clapped her hands.

"How do I look?" He wore a blue striped shirt he'd spent the better part of the day ironing and his best tan pants. Mae's daddy put his hand out, and her mama took it. He twirled her around on the linoleum.

"Look, Shelby." Mae took her sister's chin and pointed her face toward their parents. "You two should go dancing after dinner," she suggested.

"Are you kidding me? My big toe is permanently bent from when your mama stepped on it in high school."

Her mama pretended to stomp on his foot. "You were the one stepping on toes that night, Mister." Mae laughed as she watched her daddy hop around the kitchen to avoid her mama's high heels.

Out of breath, they both leaned against the counter. "We'd better stop these shenanigans before I wrinkle my shirt. Mae Ellen, let's go over—"

"I've got it, Daddy. I know the numbers. I know how to feed her. I know how to operate the TV and work the micro-wave. We'll be fine. Now go," she said, pushing her parents toward the door.

"Hang on," her mama said. She hustled back to the table and gave Shelby a quick hug. "Bye, Shelby Grace. Have fun with your sister." Then she hugged Mae. "Thank you," she whispered in Mae's ear.

"Come on, Leigh Ann. There's a hush puppy calling my name." Mae's daddy opened the front door. "Bye, girls. Don't make any crank phone calls or TP anybody's house."

Mae shook her head and waved her hands. "Shoo already."

She stood at the door and watched as they backed out of the driveway.

Mae pulled Shelby's wheelchair out from the table. "I thought they'd never leave. What do ya want to do, Shelbs? Watch TV? Sit on the front porch?" Mae walked outside to test the temperature. It was starting to cool down for the evening. The phone rang, and she ran back inside.

"Hello?" Mae answered. It was her daddy. He couldn't remember if he'd unplugged the iron. They were heading back home.

"Hang on a sec." Mae ran to the laundry closet. "You unplugged it."

"Are you sure?" he asked. "'Cause we can come home and go out another night."

"Daddy!"

"Yes, ma'am. Going to Ralph's. See you later." The phone clicked.

Mae pushed Shelby toward the door. She held the screen door open with her left foot while she moved Shelby's seat. It was hard. Mae's permanent job was to hold doors open for Shelby whenever they went somewhere. She'd never thought much about it, but now, struggling to do it all by herself, she realized how helpful it was to have her around. She got

Shelby midway through the doorframe and shifted her hip to hold the screen door open. Mae tugged on the wheelchair until she got her sister out. She put the brakes on the chair and plopped down on the porch swing.

Shelby's favorite place was outside—she loved its sights and sounds. Shelby tilted her head toward two birds chirping back and forth, and Mae pointed out a squirrel scurrying up a tree.

"Well, look who it is," Mae called when she saw Jimmy Mac riding up the driveway.

"Hey, Shelby," he said. He set his bike down and walked up the porch ramp. "Hey, Mae."

"If you're looking for cake, you might as well turn yourself right around and head back home."

"Nah, I ain't here for cake." He sat in the rocking chair next to Mae. "You still mad?"

"About what? You can't help yourself when Savanna's around."

"Don't go starting that again."

Mae rolled her eyes. "Whatever."

Jimmy Mac looked at Shelby and shook his head. "Your sister can't let things go."

Shelby clapped her hands, and Jimmy Mac laughed. "I knew you'd agree with me."

"Don't try to get her on your side," Mae said, smiling. "Wanna help with Shelby?"

"Sure!"

"Sit with her while I heat up her dinner. Shelby can eat out here on a TV tray."

Mae took the mac and cheese out of the refrigerator and warmed it in the microwave. The open kitchen door welcomed in a breeze. Mae could hear Jimmy Mac talking to her sister. Shelby loved Jimmy Mac. She held her head higher whenever he was around and seemed to look straight in his eyes whenever he talked to her.

Mae removed the top of the yogurt container and heard an ambulance siren in the distance. Her heart thumped. She gripped the counter. The siren got louder as it got closer. She wanted to bolt for the door, hop on her bike, and ride to the river. Then a different siren joined in, a fire truck this time. Mae thought her heart might jump out of her chest. She closed her eyes. She went someplace else in her head.

Mae saw herself, eyes shut tight, standing in front of nine candles, making a wish. That awful wish she should've never said. Even if it was just to herself.

The sirens got quieter, and Mae remembered where she was—in her kitchen, eleven years old. Mae turned on the faucet, the water splattering in the kitchen sink. She took a deep breath. She let it out.

"You making a pot roast in there?" Jimmy Mac shouted. "Hurry up! Shelby's hungry."

Shelby's fine, Mae told herself. For once the sirens weren't headed to her house.

She set up the TV tray on the porch in front of Shelby's chair and went back into the kitchen to put together Shelby's drink, matching the correct lid with the right cup and selecting Shelby's favorite straw. Jimmy Mac held the screen door open as she brought Shelby's supper out.

Some foods Shelby could pick up and eat on her own. Things like soggy French fries were easy to chew and swallow. And any cereal with marshmallows—Shelby loved those. But she was pretty messy with other food—missing her mouth most of the time and getting more food on her instead of in her. Usually, her parents chopped up the food real fine and fed her. That way they knew she was getting enough to eat and didn't have to constantly change her clothes.

Her parents made it look so easy, but this was the first time Mae had ever tried to feed her sister. Jimmy Mac watched over her shoulder as she scooped up yogurt and gently placed it in Shelby's mouth.

"She likes yogurt, doesn't she?" he asked.

"Strawberry-banana's her favorite." Shelby finished the entire container.

Gravel crunched on the driveway. Beecher rode his bike up first and Bubba followed. Mae and Jimmy Mac craned their necks to see Bubba, who was pulling a wagon behind his bike.

"Come on," Beecher hollered as he let his bike fall to the ground. "We ain't got all night."

"Shut up," Bubba griped. "You pull it if you're in such a hurry."

Jimmy Mac scooted back in his chair and stopped rocking, hoping to blend in with the porch and go unnoticed by both of the Duncan boys.

Mae walked down the ramp connecting the porch to the yard and put her hands on her hips. "What are you two doing here?"

"Bubba's come to make good on his bet." Beecher turned to his cousin. "Aren't ya?"

"Yeah, yeah," Bubba mumbled. "I see Tiny Mac's here."

Mae and Beecher turned and looked at the porch. Jimmy Mac gave a fake grin and a tiny wave.

"Sorry about yesterday, Mae. I tried to find him for ya." Beecher punched Bubba in the arm. "Turns out he was at some lady's trailer eating cookies."

Jimmy Mac scrunched his face, most likely worried World War III was about to break out right in Mae's front yard.

Bubba's eye twitched. Mae could tell he was thinking she'd spill the beans about baking with Miss Fannie.

But she didn't say a word. All these years Bubba had taunted her—well, it's not like Mae was completely innocent, she'd done her share of name-calling and arguing—but it didn't seem important anymore. It sort of surprised her. Maybe being nicer wasn't as hard as she thought.

Bubba looked at Mae sideways. Her silence must've surprised him too.

Mae walked around the wagon. "You actually think I'm gonna ride in this thing?"

"See. I told you this was a stupid idea," Bubba groaned to Beecher. He turned to Mae. "You don't care nothin' about that bet we made at the Hooch, do ya?"

"Mae!" Jimmy Mac shouted. "Something's wrong with Shelby!"

Mae sprinted up the ramp. Shelby's eyes were wide and watery. She was choking. "What'd you do?" Mae yelled.

"I—I gave her some macaroni and cheese. Just a tiny spoonful," Jimmy Mac said, trying not to cry.

Beecher and Bubba ran to the porch. "What's wrong with her?" Beecher asked.

Shelby's body stilled, and her eyes closed. Mae kneeled on the porch and put her cheek in front of Shelby's mouth, trying to feel if any air was coming or going. "Shelby!" Mae screamed. She looked up at Jimmy Mac. "She's not breathing."

Jimmy Mac's face turned white, and his chin began to tremble.

Mae grabbed her sister by the shoulders. "Look at me, Shelby! Look at me!"

Shelby's eyes opened, then shut again. Her head slumped to her chest.

"Do something!" Bubba shouted.

"Shelby!" Mae hugged her sister tight. For a second, she thought about that birthday two years ago. Birthday candles flickered. Wish made. Big breath. Flames blown out. That horrible wish. *I didn't mean it,* Mae shouted inside her head. *I take it back.* Mae squeezed her eyes. "Please, Shelby, breathe."

Shelby stayed in her sister's grasp, and Mae's brain rolled the tape again—the next day when she was supposed to be watching Shelby while her daddy was gone and her mama took a bath. Mae rode her new bike in the yard, and then she walked inside the house to find Shelby slumped in her chair, not breathing. Her mama screamed, her daddy dropped their dinner, and the ambulance came.

The day Shelby almost died. And Mae's ninth birthday wish almost came true. That horrible, awful wish. To be an only kid—to not have a sister.

"I'm sorry, Shelby," Mae said, tears streaming down her face. "I didn't mean it." She squeezed her sister tighter. "Please, God."

The boys looked at each other. They were silent and frozen on the porch.

Shelby coughed, and Mae loosened her hold on her sister. "She's coughing," Mae said. "Maybe air's getting through now." Shelby continued coughing, louder and harder each time. Mae lifted her cup and tried to get Shelby to suck juice through the straw, but Shelby wouldn't hold her head still. Shelby's leg jerked like a spasm.

"Do something, Mae!" Bubba hollered.

"She's having a seizure. Help me get her out of the chair and on her side," Mae ordered.

Jimmy Mac held the wheelchair still as Mae lifted under Shelby's arms. Beecher guided her torso, and Bubba lowered Shelby's legs to the floor. Mae held Shelby's head in her lap, turning it slightly so she wouldn't choke on her spit. Mae watched Shelby's chest rise and fall with each breath.

"Everybody, stay calm," she said. Mae wiped her face with her arm. "Jimmy Mac, call 911."

Jimmy Mac ran inside, grabbed the cordless phone, and hurried back to the front porch. He punched in the numbers and knelt beside Mae. He pushed the speaker button so that everyone could hear. They all exchanged nervous glances as they waited for the operator to answer.

"What time is it?" Mae asked.

Beecher looked at his watch. "Five-thirty. Why?"

"We've got to time the seizure and tell the paramedics."

"911. What's your emergency?" they finally heard.

"I'm at Mae Moore's house. Her sister's having a seizure or something. We need you to send an ambulance."

"Is that you, Jimmy Mac?" the operator asked.

"Miss Peggy?" he asked. Miss Peggy was a substitute teacher at the school, subbing when she was off from her dispatch job. She was one of the nice subs. She ignored the seating chart and gave the class ten extra minutes at recess.

"Is she breathing?"

Jimmy Mac looked at Mae. She nodded.

"Yes," he said.

"Good. Can you get her on her side?" the operator asked.

"She already is. Please hurry."

"You're doing great, Jimmy Mac," Miss Peggy said. "Keep her from hurting herself, and I'll send someone when I can."

Mae leaned toward the phone, "How long?"

"There's been a major accident involving the train and at least two cars. My ambulances and the fire truck are at the scene." She paused. "I don't have anyone who can come to you right now. Hang on a sec—one of the paramedics is on the radio."

Mae looked at the boys as she held Shelby's head in her lap. She wondered if she had the same look of panic on her face as they did.

"What's taking so long?" Bubba asked.

Jimmy Mac placed his hand over the receiver and said, "She's talking to somebody on the radio." Jimmy Mac stood and turned the speaker off.

"Yes, ma'am." He held the phone to his ear. Miss Peggy was back on.

Mae's eyes shifted between Shelby and Jimmy Mac. He walked down, then back up the ramp. "But they'll come after that, right?" he asked.

Mae got a sick feeling in her stomach.

Jimmy Mac swallowed hard. "Yes, ma'am. Thank you." He clicked the phone off.

"What'd she say?" Bubba asked. "When they getting here?"

Jimmy Mac looked at his shoes.

"They're not coming, are they?" Mae asked.

He shook his head. "They can't get anyone here for a while. Miss Peggy said there were injuries, and one of the train cars derailed. It was carrying fertilizer. If it catches fire—it's not good."

"A train wreck," Mae said under her breath. Shelby's leg continued to twitch from the seizure. Mae put her hand on her sister's shoulder. "Don't worry, Shelby. I'm here."

"You all right, Bubba?" Beecher asked his cousin. Bubba slouched in a rocker and nodded his head. "Bubba's daddy was hit by a train," Beecher said, not realizing Mae and Jimmy Mac already knew.

Bubba looked up. "It was right before I was born. My daddy and Preacher Floyd's son."

"The preacher's son?" Jimmy Mac asked.

"It was early one morning. Still dark out. They'd just left the factory." Bubba stopped for a minute. "Mama said Daddy was in a hurry to get home. I was coming soon. He didn't want to miss it."

Mae's mama had told her the story a few years back, hoping she'd cut him some slack on account of his daddy. It was after Mae had complained about Bubba for the billionth time. Her mama had explained the Jessup Fire Department was run by volunteers back then, and the town had only one fire truck. An ambulance had to come from the next county because Butler County Memorial Hospital hadn't been built yet.

She had said the volunteer firefighters couldn't get to Bubba Senior or his passenger—the truck was too mangled. Gasoline had spilled everywhere, and the firefighters did everything they could, but the truck and two train cars went up in flames.

Mae hadn't realized the passenger had been Preacher Floyd's son. "I don't know why bad things happen to good people," Mae remembered the preacher saying. He had lost his own son.

Shelby was still. The seizure had finally ended. Mae gently brushed her sister's hair from her face. She looked at Beecher's watch. It was five thirty-six. *Six minutes.* She committed the length of her sister's seizure to memory. "I need to call my parents," she said. "They're at Ralph's on the River."

Jimmy Mac handed her the phone, and she punched in her mama's cell number.

All eyes were on Mae. She clicked the phone off. "It went straight to voicemail," she said. "I'll try Daddy." Seconds later, when he didn't answer, she said, "They always answer their phones."

"Call Ralph's," Bubba suggested.

"Good thinking," Mae said. "The number's hanging in the kitchen by the phone."

Jimmy Mac ran for the door. "I'll get it!" The screen door slammed behind him. Lickety-split, he was back, handing Mae the notebook paper with the restaurant's number.

"Ralph's on the River. How can I help you?" the man asked.

"I need Leigh and Gary Ann Moore!" she shouted into the phone.

"Come again?" he said.

Calm down, Mae thought. "Gary and Leigh Ann Moore. My parents. They're eating there. It's an emergency," she said, accentuating each syllable.

"Hang on. We're not too crowded yet," the man said.

"I ain't never been to Ralph's," Bubba said. Jimmy Mac raised both eyebrows.

"Who's Ralph?" Beecher asked. Jimmy Mac lifted his finger to his lips, pointing to Shelby.

"The seizure's over. She's sleeping now," Mae told Jimmy Mac and the other boys. "She's worn out."

The man returned to the phone. "The servers and I have gone to every table, and there isn't anyone here by that name. Are you sure they were coming to Ralph's?"

"Yes, sir."

"I'll keep asking the customers as they come in. If they're here, they'll get the message."

"Thank you," she said. Mae put the phone down and rubbed her forehead. It didn't make any sense. "They should have been there by now," she said. "They left a long time ago."

Mae and Jimmy Mac locked eyes. It was as if they had the same thought, but neither of them wanted to say it out loud. *The train. An accident. Injuries. Fire.*

Mae couldn't let herself think about that. An ambulance wasn't coming. And now there was no way to reach her parents. There were only a few houses on her street, and the neighbors to the left and right were away on vacation. "Jimmy Mac, go across the street and see if anybody's home. Their car's not out, but go check."

Jimmy Mac ran as fast as he could and rang the doorbell. He looked back at Mae and the others on the porch across the street. Jimmy Mac pounded on the door. Nothing. He ran back, almost completely out of breath, and said, "Nobody. Home."

Mae sighed loudly. It was up to her to take care of her sister. "We've got to get Shelby to the hospital. The seizure's over, but it lasted a long time."

"But you heard Jimmy Mac," Beecher said. "Ain't nobody coming, and nobody's at home."

"That's why I said 'we,'" Mae said. "Bubba, do you think your wagon can hold her?"

"It'll hold her," Bubba answered. "Beecher and me took turns carting each other around the trailer park when we were bored last week."

Jimmy Mac bit his lip. The boys were at least two times the weight of Shelby, but pulling her to the hospital? "I don't know, Mae. I think we should wait here," Jimmy Mac said.

"Wait for what? And for how long? I can't just sit here and not get her help. What if she stops breathing again? Or has another seizure?" Mae couldn't stand the thought. She looked at Bubba. "Go in the living room and grab the blanket off the back of the couch. Beecher, get some rope from the garage. It's hanging on the back wall," Mae ordered.

Beecher and Bubba did as they were told. Mae knew Jimmy Mac disagreed with her plan. "If we see a car along the way, we'll flag them down. But—"

"I know. You can't just sit here and wait." Jimmy Mac said. There was no sense trying to talk her out of it.

CHAPTER SIXTEEN

Bubba padded the bottom of the wagon with the blanket and walked his bike close to the porch ramp. They gently lifted Shelby and placed her in the wagon. She was longer than the wagon's length, so they bent her knees and tucked her legs in. Beecher and Mae zigzagged the rope back and forth across the tall sides of the wagon so that she'd be secure if the wagon hit a bump.

Bubba straddled his bike when Mae put her hands on his handlebars. "No, Bubba. She's my sister. I'll pull her."

"You sure?" Bubba asked.

"I'm sure. You can ride mine."

"Okay, but the hospital's at least two miles. I can take a turn if you get tired," Bubba said.

"We all can," Beecher added.

Mae got on Bubba's bike and pushed down on the pedal. It was hard. His seat was higher than hers. It took some getting used to, but she got into a slow rhythm by the time she reached the end of her drive.

The weight of the wagon and Shelby made pedaling difficult, but Mae pressed, one pedal at a time, alternating between standing and sitting. She was flanked by Bubba and Beecher on each side, with Jimmy Mac close behind. All four of them gained speed as they continued pedaling, hoping to see a car.

There was no way Mae would have been strong enough to do something like this last summer, but climbing the steep hill on the way to Hopewell Church had strengthened her leg muscles. It was as if riding to drive-thru prayer, even just a few times, had gotten her ready for this night.

They rested a couple of minutes at the four-way stop on Winder Street. Surely a car would pass by. But none did. "Where is everybody?" Beecher asked.

Mae wondered if everyone was at the accident, their cars lined up near the train tracks, watching the scary scene.

"Want me to take a turn?" Beecher asked.

"It's not so hard," Mae answered. "I'm used to it now."

The two-wheeled caravan started up again. They all turned left to go down Winder—except Jimmy Mac.

Bubba yelled at him, "C'mon. We can't slow down now!"

Jimmy Mac turned his bike and hollered, "I've got to—I'll—sorry, Mae." And he rode in the opposite direction without looking back.

"Where's he going?" Beecher asked.

Mae watched him ride away and felt her heart drop with each of his pedal strokes. "Let's go," she ordered. "We don't need him." Only, she was thinking, *Why would he leave me when I need him most?*

———

Mae pedaled as if she weren't pulling any extra weight. She looked back every now and again to check on Shelby, who was safely tucked in the wagon and not making any movement or sounds.

"Hey! Is that Mrs. Willene?" Bubba asked. There was no mistaking the blue Buick. It took up most of the road. They waited until she got closer before they waved their arms in the air like they were trying to flag down an airplane.

"Scoot over, she's coming fast!" Mae shouted. They moved their bikes and the wagon farther off the road. As she passed them, Mrs. Willene stuck her arm out her window and waved.

"Did she just pass right by us?" Beecher asked. All three turned their heads and watched as she went down the road. She veered into the center turn lane, then swerved back.

Mae and the boys mounted their bikes and continued on. The hospital was only a mile away now, and the closer it got, the faster they pedaled.

"Look, Mae!" Bubba shouted. "How'd they know we were coming?"

Mae looked ahead and saw people standing outside the hospital—nurses, doctors, and stretchers. She pedaled hard the last seventy yards or so.

They pulled up where it said, "AMBULANCES ONLY." A nurse approached them. "You can't park here," she said. "We've got to keep this area clear for the accident victims."

Mae put her feet on the ground and pointed to the wagon. "My sister needs help."

The nurse looked in. "Get a gurney over here!" she yelled, motioning with her hand. Two men in blue scrubs hurried one to her. "What happened?" the nurse asked as they carefully lifted Shelby out of the wagon.

Mae followed them inside the hospital and explained Shelby had choked on mac and cheese and then seized. They turned down a long hallway where another nurse approached them. "It's Shelby Moore. I'll call Dr. Gordon," the nurse said. Mae recognized her from the times Shelby had been in the hospital before.

Mae could no longer keep up with the pace of the nurses or the men pushing Shelby. She was exhausted from the ride, the weight of the wagon, and the worry of her sister. "Six minutes!" Mae yelled at them. "The seizure lasted six minutes." One of the nurses turned back to her. "You did good," she said. "We'll take care of your sister." She disappeared with Shelby through another set of doors.

Mae leaned against the hospital wall. Her legs couldn't hold her up any longer, and she started to slide to the floor.

Ever since the nurse had given Bubba and Beecher a keep-out-of-the-way look when they were outside, they'd kept their distance. But as soon as they saw Mae hit the wall, they rushed to her. The boys caught her arms and half dragged, half carried her to a chair in the waiting room.

"She needs something to drink. Give me some money for the vending machine," Bubba barked at Beecher.

"I ain't got any money," Beecher answered.

Bubba looked around the waiting area and saw a lone older gentleman sitting there. The man pointed to a water fountain with a cup dispenser beside it. Bubba raced to it.

Bubba handed Mae the cup of water, and he and Beecher watched as she drank. Then the cousins ran to the fountain, filled their cups, and gulped the water down. They did it three more times, dribbling water down the front of their shirts. The kids sat in the hospital's hard plastic, scoop-bottomed chairs, exhausted.

The large hospital front doors opened, and Davis Hampton walked in.

"There you are," he said, approaching Mae. "You all right?"

Mae nodded, glad someone in the adult-age range had finally joined them. "I can't get a hold of my parents." Mae gave a puzzled look. "How'd you know I was here?"

"Your friend."

"Huh?" she asked.

"Never mind that now," Davis said. "I gotta tell you something."

They watched as a nurse pushed the button on the wall to keep the hospital doors open. Davis continued, "About your parents. They were—"

He was interrupted by an ambulance siren that floated in from outside. Mae closed her eyes and breathed in a huge breath. She knew her parents were in it.

CHAPTER SEVENTEEN

D avis and Mae ran outside, followed by Beecher and Bubba. The hospital workers were still there, waiting to receive the injured.

Mae had hoped, prayed even, that her parents were safe at Ralph's, all the while knowing something was wrong when neither of them answered their phones.

An ambulance pulled into the entrance. And another. Then a third. They watched as an organized mob of hospital workers met each one.

Mae leaped forward, and Davis grabbed her elbow to keep her back. "You should wait inside. I'll find out what's going on and let you know," he told her.

Mae shook her arm free. "I need to see my parents."

With Bubba and Beecher trailing close behind, Mae and Davis moved closer to the first ambulance as its doors opened. The paramedics lowered a stretcher with a man on it. He wore a blue bandana on his head, and tattoos covered his left arm. He was sitting up, his right arm wrapped in white gauze.

They hurried to the second ambulance and peered between the workers moving frantically to attend to the second patient. It was another man. His head was wrapped in a bloodied bandage, but he was conscious and talking to the nurse beside him.

"Where are they?" Mae asked. They raced down the sidewalk to the last ambulance. The doors swung open, and, as Mae stretched her neck to see, a large man dressed in blue scrubs stepped in front of her.

Bubba and Beecher stood frozen beside Mae. Her heart pounded. "Is it them?" she asked Davis.

As the huge man stepped aside, Mae saw her mama climb out. Mae ran to her and hugged her, almost tackling her from behind. "Mae Ellen, how'd you—" She looked at Davis, then Bubba and Beecher.

Ricky and James pulled out the stretcher with Mae's daddy on it. His left foot and ankle were wrapped. Mae looked him over toe to head and back again. She exhaled, relieved things weren't worse.

"Where's Shelby Grace?" he asked when he saw Mae.

"She's inside," Mae said. "The nurse says she'll be fine."

"Nurse?" Mae's mama and daddy shouted together.

"Wait'll you hear this story, Mr. Moore," Davis said, following them into the hospital.

Once they were inside, Mae remembered Bubba and Beecher. They could leave now and get home before Bubba's mama called them in for supper. Mae watched them through the glass doors.

Beecher and Bubba stood alone on the sidewalk—their natural color slowly replaced the ghostly hue that had been on their faces since Shelby's seizure on the porch. Beecher hugged his cousin until Bubba realized what they were doing. Bubba dropped his arms and tried to wiggle free. "Let go of me, you big baby!"

Beecher turned him loose, then play-punched him in the arm.

Mae smiled and shook her head. *Who would've ever figured?* she thought.

CHAPTER EIGHTEEN

The next morning, the doctor came in early to check on Mae's daddy and sister. They had all spent the night in the same hospital room as Shelby, where she was recovering from her seizure. Mae's daddy was waiting to hear if he needed surgery or just a boot to help his ankle mend.

Mae's mama sat on the edge of Shelby's hospital bed, keeping watch over her. The doctor had said she'd be just fine, but her body was, in his words, "plum tuckered out."

Mae tried to rub out the crick in her neck she'd gotten from sleeping in the chair when there was a knock on the door.

Davis peeked in. "You folks taking visitors?" He walked in, holding a white box. "I brought cookies from Miss Fannie."

"We're taking visitors bearing gifts from Fannie," Mae's daddy said. "Have a seat."

Mae hopped up. "I'll take those off your hands," she said, taking the box from Davis.

"I can't stay long." Davis glanced at Shelby, then Mae's daddy.

"Shelby Grace is resting," Mae's daddy said. "She's doing good."

Davis sat. "I went by the grocery store this morning—" He turned to Mae's mama. "Mr. Adams says to take as long as you need." She nodded and smiled. Davis continued, "Anyway, I stopped to get a donut and coffee when Miss Fannie asked if I'd drop these off to y'all."

Mae's daddy scooted over in his bed to see inside the box. Mae handed him a cookie. "Best medicine around," he said. He took a bite and swallowed. "Listen, we appreciate you looking after Mae yesterday."

Davis turned to Mae. "She did fine on her own. By the time I went looking for her, she'd already towed her sister all the way here."

Mae's cheeks turned red, and she looked at the floor tiles. She was uncomfortable with the attention. Plus, she figured she'd done what anyone would've done if their sister was in trouble.

Yesterday's ride flashed in her mind. She remembered looking back at Shelby in the wagon. It seemed like a nightmare. But it had happened, and Mae had been Shelby's only hope of getting to the hospital. Mae was still exhausted.

Mae cocked her head. "How'd you know I was pulling Shelby?"

"Jimmy Mac." Davis eyed the box.

"Jimmy Mac?" she asked.

Davis stood and reached toward the box. "Mind if I—"

Mae passed him the cookies.

"Yeah, he rode to the church and told us." He explained, stuffing a cookie in his mouth.

The church? Mae figured he'd gone home, tired of riding or scared about his part in Shelby needing to go to the hospital in the first place.

But when Jimmy Mac had left Mae and the others on Winder Street, he'd ridden to the church. That was even farther than the hospital. Then she remembered yesterday was Thursday, drive-thru prayer day. "He told you and Preacher Floyd?" she asked, taking the box back.

"Us, Miss Fannie, his mama—heck, pretty much the whole town was there. Everybody heard about the accident. They'd all gone to the train tracks to see if they could help, but the police had blocked the road and turned them away. So they went to the church."

Mrs. Twila got out of bed, Mae thought.

"Jimmy Mac flew down Hopewell's driveway, and when he spotted his mama, he threw his bike down, shouting something about hurting your sister." Davis glanced at Shelby. "He said she was bad off on account of him, and you were towing her to the hospital."

Mae started to feel guilty about the thoughts she'd had, assuming Jimmy Mac had ditched her when she needed him most. *I should have known he'd never do that,* she thought.

Davis looked at his watch, then sat on the edge of the chair. "What happened at the train crossing yesterday?"

Mae's daddy proceeded to tell Davis what he'd already told Mae last night, right before the doctor shot him full of pain medication, and he went out like a light. "It was a matter of being in the wrong place at the wrong time," he said, shaking his head.

"Or the right place at the right time," Mae's mama added.

"Guess it depends on who you ask," he said. "We were headed to Ralph's on the River, courtesy of you-know-who . . ." he nodded to Mae ". . . when we got behind a big white van. One of them vans with every inch covered in advertisements. Like somebody'd painted a billboard, then wrapped it around a van."

Davis gave a puzzled look.

"Said 'Flip-Flops,' or something like that," Mae's daddy said.

Mae's mama shook her head. "It said, 'Let us flip your flop.'"

"House fixer-uppers," Mae said, stuffing another cookie in her mouth.

"Renovators," Mae's daddy said, nodding. "We were behind them for a good five or six miles, and I could tell they were lost. They'd slow down, then speed up, then slow down again, trying to figure out which turn to take."

"Probably from Atlanta," Mae added.

"You know it," her daddy said.

Mae smiled big, showing chocolate stuck to her teeth. Davis muffled a chuckle.

Mae's daddy continued, "I was getting kind of nervous 'cause we were getting close to the train crossing at Puckett's Road." He stopped for a minute and shook his head. "Jessup has been after Southern Rails for going on eleven years now to fix that crossing. They've never had any gates, and the red flashing lights only work half the time."

Davis nodded. Everybody in town knew that train crossing. It's where two people had died, Bubba's daddy and—Mae now knew the other person—the preacher's son.

"Darn if that van didn't pull right up on the edge of the tracks and stop." Her daddy shifted and grimaced at the pain. He lifted his foot while Mae's mama adjusted the pillow propped under his ankle.

Mae saw Davis glance at his watch again. He tapped his foot on the floor. Something was up. Did he have somewhere to be?

"I put the car in park and walked up to the driver's window," Mae's daddy continued. "I asked if he'd ever seen a railroad crossing sign before, and if not, to take a look at the one right outside his window."

"Please tell me you didn't say that," Mae's mama said, looking like she did the time she'd walked down the bread aisle at the Piggly Wiggly and discovered she had toilet paper stuck to her shoe.

Mae's daddy acted like he didn't hear her. "The driver was fiddling with some buttons on a screen, and the passenger was looking at his phone, both trying to figure out where in tarnation they were."

Mae turned to Davis. "Right there on the train tracks," she said.

"Let's move this story along, you two," Mae's mama said, noticing Davis was getting antsy. "I'm sure Davis has other things to do."

"Are you delivering cookies to other patients?" Mae asked, grinning.

Davis's shoulders slumped. "Great, now the town will think I'm the Piggly Wiggly delivery boy." He sighed loudly.

"They could think a whole lot of worse things." The words slipped out of Mae's mouth, and Davis looked at her. She wondered if Davis agreed—being hooked on drugs was way worse than being a delivery boy—even if neither one was true. Mae's daddy squinted at the two of them. It was like Davis had a secret, and Mae was the only one who knew about it.

"All right, I'll get to the exciting part," Mae's daddy continued. "I told them to pull up, and I'd give 'em directions, but 'for Pete's sake, get off the train tracks!' The driver put the van in drive, but it wouldn't move. The engine had died. And now we hear—"

"A train coming?" Davis asked.

"Exactly." Mae's daddy shifted in the bed again. It was hard for him to sit too long in one spot. "I told them to get out of the van, but the driver said the equipment inside was too expensive to let it get smashed to smithereens."

Davis and Mae's mama shook their heads.

"The train was getting way too close for comfort, and the engineer was blowing the whistle like crazy. The passenger tried to open his door, but the lock wouldn't unlock. It was like the van's electrical system just shut down. So I ran back to our car and yelled at Leigh Ann to get out."

Mae's mama jumped in the conversation. "I didn't know what he was gonna do. He kept yelling, 'Get out of the car! Get out of the car!'"

"As soon as she was out, I drove my front bumper into the van's back bumper and tried to push the van. But it only moved a little and was now sitting smack in the middle of the train tracks. We were running out of time."

"My heart's racing just thinking about it." Mae's mama put her hand on her chest. "The engineer tried to slow down, but there wasn't enough time to come to a stop."

"How fast do you think it was going?" Davis asked.

"Had to be about forty miles an hour," Mae's daddy said. "It was gonna take more than a push to get the van off the tracks, so I backed up, shoved the car into drive again, and rammed the back of the van as hard as I could." Mae's daddy looked at his propped-up foot. "I twisted up my ankle pretty good doing it, but it did the trick. The van smashed into a big oak tree on the side of the road, and the train clipped my back bumper."

"The two fellas were pretty banged up, but it coulda been a lot worse," her daddy continued. "We only found out one of the train cars was loaded with fertilizer when the fire trucks arrived, and they aimed all their water hoses at it."

"Wow," Davis said, shaking his head. "Glad y'all are all right." He stood and adjusted his baseball cap. "I reckon I'd better get going."

"Where you headed?" Mae asked.

"Mae!" her mama shouted. "Stop being nosy." Mae's face turned red, but she wanted to know. And by the way Davis skedaddled out of the hospital room, he didn't want to say.

Mae's daddy settled in for a nap, and her mama decided it was time to take Mae home so that they could clean up. They were gathering their things when someone knocked.

"What is it, Halloween? We don't have this many visitors come to the house," Mae's daddy said, propping himself up. Mae scrambled to open the door.

A man with a cast on his arm walked in. "Sorry to bother you, but I wanted to say thanks," he said, looking at Mae's daddy. Mae recognized the tattoos on his arm. He was one of the guys from the ambulances yesterday.

The man stuck out his good hand to Mae's daddy. "I believe we've met," her daddy said, "but not formally. I'm Gary Moore."

"I'm Jace and my brother's Cam." He shook hands with Mae's mama next. "We're the Gilbert brothers." He said it like Mae and her parents were supposed to know that already.

Mae's parents looked at each other.

"From *Flip This Flop*," he said.

Her parents narrowed their eyes.

"The TV show," he added.

"Oh," Mae's mama said. "Never seen it."

Mae picked up the box of Miss Fannie's cookies and walked them over to the visitor. "Daddy says if we had an extra thirty dollars a month, we wouldn't blow it on trash TV."

"Mae Ellen!" her mama hollered.

Jace laughed and reached in to get a cookie. "That's all right, ma'am. We're not everybody's cup of tea."

"Please." Mae's daddy pointed to the chair. "How's your brother?"

Jace took a last bite of cookie, then licked his fingers. "He's got a huge gash on his head," he said, drawing a line on the front of his scalp with his finger. "It took twenty stitches to sew him up, but he'll be fine."

"What brought you two to Jessup?" Mae's mama asked.

Jace explained how he and his brother bought rundown properties and then renovated them, filling them with new appliances, furniture—whatever was needed to make them better than new. He said the show's executive producer had seen an advertisement about an auction in Jessup.

"The Donut Hole?" Mae asked.

"Yeah," Jace said. He looked in the cookie box, then at Mae.

"Help yourself," she said. Mae realized she'd been wrong, thinking Savanna's mama had bought the place. "You and your brother bought it?"

"We did." Jace took another cookie. "Most of the time on *Flip This Flop*, we buy a property, redo it, then sell it for a profit." He looked at Mae's daddy. "We're pretty good at it. But the producers wanted to do something different to celebrate our fiftieth episode."

Jace explained how they planned to spend an entire season helping out folks in towns that were down on their luck. Jessup would be the first of several. They'd planned to give The Donut Hole a makeover, then sell it to somebody in the town at below cost. That way the owners could start their own business, and Jessup would benefit too.

There was another knock at the door. Mae opened it and let another man in.

"I figured you'd be here." He walked toward Mae's daddy and shook his hand. "Cam Gilbert. I appreciate all you did yesterday. And we'll take care of those dents to your car."

"You're welcome, and we appreciate that," her daddy said.

Cam turned to his brother. "Listen, we got a phone call from somebody wanting to make an offer on the place."

"Already?" Jace asked. "We haven't even started renovating yet."

Cam turned his head, and Mae could see a shaved part where the stitches lay underneath a bandage. He sniffed the air. "I smell chocolate."

"Triple Cs," Mae said, offering him the box.

Cam took a cookie. "Someone named Weatherall." He took a bite. "You folks know them?"

Mae twisted her lips. "I've heard of 'em."

Her daddy laughed.

"Gosh, these are good," Cam said. He reached back inside the box, but it was empty.

Jace looked over his brother's shoulder. "You ate the last one?" he asked, flicking his brother's arm.

"Ow," Cam hollered. "How many did you have before I got here?"

Mae's parents laughed at the brothers while Mae's mind set to thinking.

The Gilbert brothers said more thank-yous, then good-byes, as they headed for the door.

Mae hopped up. "What would you say if I told you that you could get an unlimited supply of those cookies?" Mae asked.

Cam and Jace turned back around. "We'd say, 'Tell us more,'" Jace said, smiling.

CHAPTER NINETEEN

Three cookies were all it took to convince the Gilbert brothers that Miss Fannie Higgins deserved a chance at getting the new and improved Donut Hole. Like Preacher Floyd once said, "Sometimes your prayers get answered in ways you never expected."

But it wasn't like they could just give the property to Miss Fannie, not with Mrs. Weatherall offering to buy it first.

After Mae told the brothers about Miss Fannie's money problems and how having her own bakery could help her support herself, they said they'd go back to their room and think on a way to give both ladies a fair shot at owning their own business.

An hour later, they were back. "So how would folks in Jessup feel about an old-fashioned bake sale?" Cam asked.

"How do you mean?" Mae's mama asked.

Jace looked at his brother, then Mae's parents. "We think our viewers would be interested in a competition."

"Right," Cam followed up. "Both ladies would have four hours to bake and sell. Each one can have one assistant. Whoever sold the most homemade products would win The Donut Hole."

"And our promise to renovate the place to their specifications," Jace explained.

Mae smiled big. "Miss Fannie could finally have her own bakery."

"Slow down. You know Alice Weatherall," her daddy said. He turned to the brothers. "You're talking about a David versus Goliath match-up."

Mae frowned. She knew what he was saying. Then she raised her eyebrows. "But David won," she said.

The Gilbert brothers looked at each other and smiled. Jace and Cam explained they'd go ahead and put in new countertops, two bakery-style ovens, and a huge refrigerator the two could use during their baking. Then they'd sell their goodies outside on the sidewalk, just like a regular bake sale.

"We want to get folks excited about The Donut Hole—or whatever the winner will call it—getting a new life," Jace added.

"Jessup could use a little excitement," Mae's daddy said. "A new shop would revitalize downtown, boost the economy."

Mae nodded enthusiastically, even though she wasn't exactly sure what he meant.

"Hang on," her mama said. "Has anyone bothered to ask Fannie if she wants to take on a bakery? Or Alice Weatherall?"

Mae looked up at the ceiling.

"Mae Ellen?" her daddy asked.

Jace and Cam looked at Mae.

Mae hadn't exactly gotten Miss Fannie's agreement on the own-your-own-bakery idea. *Surely, Miss Fannie would want her own bakery, right?* Mae wondered. *And this competition is the only way to get it.* Mae took a deep breath. "I'll work on that," she said.

Mae's mama gave her an uncertain look. She worked with Miss Fannie. She knew she might feel overwhelmed, especially about going up against Mrs. Weatherall.

"We'll work out the rules," Cam said. "I'm thinking each lady can have one assistant to help make the goods and up to three people to help sell the items."

"We need to get in there tomorrow," Jace told his brother. "Start tearing out the old stuff." The brothers stood and moved toward the door. "Let's see if we can get the camera crew here by Thursday," Cam added, opening the door.

Mae grabbed the top of her head. "That's in four days!"

"We're expected in Alabama next," Cam said. "We've got to get this show on the road."

The Gilbert brothers left, and Mae's parents looked at her. They didn't have to say anything. She knew what they were thinking, *Mae, you might've opened your mouth too wide this time.*

———

That afternoon, Mae's daddy and Shelby were back home. Except for Mae's daddy in a clunky boot, things were getting back to normal for the Moore family. For everyone but Mae, that is. She had her biggest challenge yet. A three-parter this time. Part 1: Get Miss Fannie to agree to participate in the bake sale. Part 2: Find her an assistant. Part 3: Make sure Miss Fannie sells more than Savanna's mama. No sweat. Only she was sweating like a turkey on the day before Thanksgiving.

Mae tried to think up a plan as she rode her bike to the Piggly Wiggly. The problem was Miss Fannie had never ventured much outside the grocery store. She was painfully shy to most folks unless you were a regular customer. She was confident behind the grocery bakery counter, but getting her to show off her baking skills in front of the whole town *and* a camera? It'd be like Mae trying to push the Gilbert brothers' van off the train tracks with her bike.

And there was that other thing—her teeth. Miss Fannie was self-conscious that her front teeth were missing.

By the time she got to the store's bench, Mae still didn't have a strategy to convince Miss Fannie to be in the bake sale.

Jimmy Mac soon rode up and sat beside her. The last time they'd seen each other was at the stop sign on Winder Street when they parted ways. Thanks to Davis, Mae now knew why he'd left her. But she liked to watch him squirm.

He cleared his throat, started to say something, then stopped. He tapped his fingers on the seat of the bench. Mae turned away, afraid her face would give her away.

He scratched his head. Then he picked at the paint chipping off the bench and whistled for a while. Jimmy Mac was a horrible whistler. Only air blew past his lips.

"You must be pretty mad," Jimmy Mac finally said. "But I can explain."

"Explain what?" Mae crossed her arms. "Why you ditched me and Shelby on the side of the road? Bubba Duncan and his cousin didn't leave me. I guess they're my best friends now." Mae turned away. She turned her lips in and bit down, trying not to smile.

"You mean it?" he asked. Only he didn't say it like he was disappointed. He said it like he was happy.

Mae looked at him. "Huh?"

"You mean you and Bubba are friends?" he asked, sounding all excited. He was talking like he'd fallen off his bike and hit his head one too many times. This was not going the way Mae had hoped.

"Nooooo," she said. "What I mean is your leaving me the other day has churned up a hate in my heart bigger than you've ever seen."

Jimmy Mac pressed his back into the bench and sighed.

Mae couldn't hold it in any longer. She burst out laughing.

"You ain't mad at me?"

"No. Davis told me what you did. Riding all the way to the church to pray for Shelby."

"Did he tell you everybody in town was already there?" he asked.

"He said your mama was even there."

"Can you believe it?"

Mae nodded her head. She was beginning to believe all sorts of things.

"Mama said when she heard about the train wreck, she decided other people had troubles worse than hers," Jimmy Mac said. "She knew she couldn't do nothin' about the accident, but she could get out of her pj's and drive to Hopewell." Jimmy Mac shuffled his feet under the bench. "How's Shelby?"

"She's fine. It wasn't your fault, you know."

He lowered his head and shook it. "I never should have given her the mac and cheese."

"She's had seizures before. It's either that or breathing problems that bring the ambulance to the house. I can't believe we put her in Bubba Duncan's wagon and towed her all the way to the hospital," Mae said.

"Did Mrs. Hampton really drive past you?"

"Only after she almost drove *over* us," Mae replied.

"That's pretty crazy," Jimmy Mac said.

"I might be able to top it." Mae told him about the Gilbert brothers coming to the hospital, eating Miss Fannie's cookies, and offering to host a bake sale competition on their TV show.

"They bought The Donut Hole?"

Mae nodded.

"And now Miss Fannie might get it?" Jimmy Mac asked.

Mae nodded again. "They said her cookies were the best they'd ever eaten." She grinned big. "So they came up with the whole bake sale idea."

"It's a miracle," Jimmy Mac said.

"I know. And now we're gonna need another one to get Miss Fannie to agree to it."

The two of them tried to think of just the right words to convince Miss Fannie. One of them started to say something, then decided it was a dumb plan and not worth saying out loud. Then the other one did the same.

They watched Davis as he drove his truck around to the side parking lot. Mae and Jimmy Mac looked at each other, wondering if three heads were better than two. Besides, Davis was once a celebrity. He might know how to talk Miss Fannie into the competition.

Davis wore his sunglasses with his hat pulled down low. He walked right past Mae and Jimmy Mac.

Mae cleared her throat. Davis stopped. "Oh, hi," he said. "What are you two up to?"

"We're trying to think up—"

Mae kicked Jimmy Mac's leg under the bench so that he'd stop talking.

Something was wrong with Davis. He was acting funny—like he was there but not paying attention to what or who was in front of him.

"Got a minute?" she asked. "We could use some help."

Davis looked at his watch. "Not really," he said. "I'm meeting somebody at the—I need to be somewhere."

Mae narrowed her eyes. *Just who did he think he was?* she wondered. She was a somebody. Somebody who remembered his past, knew about his failures, and hoped he'd make a comeback. And now she needed a favor. Miss Fannie needed a favor.

Davis sighed. "I'll give you two minutes," he said, sitting on the edge of the bench next to her.

Mae got down to business. "You love Miss Fannie's cookies, right?"

Davis looked straight ahead and nodded.

"And you care about Miss Fannie, too, don't ya?"

Davis turned to Mae. "What is this, twenty questions? 'Cause you're eating up your time."

Jimmy Mac saw Mae's jaw clench and nudged her with his elbow.

She sighed loudly. Mae straightened up on the bench, cracked a few knuckles on each hand, and took a deep breath.

"These two brothers named Jace and Cam who are the stars of *Flip This Flop*—that's a show on cable so you might not have heard of it—bought The Donut Hole and said whoever—Miss Fannie or Mrs. Weatherall—sells the most stuff, with the help of an assistant—will get The Donut Hole, completely redone, as their very own business. And, well, this is a once-in-a-lifetime opportunity that Miss Fannie doesn't know about yet—and she probably won't like the part where the brothers will have a camera and show the competition on their *Flip This Flop* show, but she doesn't need to know that part right away—and we need somebody to help convince her that she *has* got to do this." Mae took a full, deep breath.

Jimmy Mac turned away from Davis and laughed.

Mae cocked her head. "Fast enough for you?"

Davis nodded, then turned toward Mae. "Let me get this straight. If Miss Fannie sells more cookies than Mrs. Weatherall, she'll get her own bakery. Completely free?"

"Yep," said Mae. "Only Mrs. Weatherall will probably sell peach cobbler, but that's not important."

Davis was quiet. "Miss Fannie's not one to seek the spotlight," he finally said.

"She might, if it meant she could own her bakery and solve her money problems once and for all," Mae added. She looked at Davis out of the corner of her eye, hoping he'd get on board with the idea.

"I guess you're gonna be her assistant in the contest?" Davis asked Mae.

"No. I'm no good in the kitchen."

Davis raised an eyebrow and pointed to Jimmy Mac. Mae said, "Jimmy Mac's prone to accidents. He'd likely burn down The Donut Hole." She turned to Jimmy Mac. "No offense."

"None taken," Jimmy Mac said.

Davis stood. He walked in front of the grocery store doors and waited for them to open. "You work on finding her an assistant, and I'll work on Miss Fannie."

"Divvy it up. I like it," Mae said. "Find a way to convince her that it don't matter how she looks, only how she tastes."

Davis gave her a confused look.

"You know what I mean," she said.

"But after this, I'm done," Davis said. "I've got to focus on getting my life back."

"I promise," she said, making an X across her heart. "This is the last favor."

Davis walked inside the store, and Jimmy Mac saw the crossed fingers on Mae's hand tucked behind her back.

"He doesn't mean it," Mae said.

Mae and Jimmy Mac had never thought they'd ever step foot inside Bubba's trailer, but here they were, sitting on his crushed-potato-chipped couch. Bubba listened without saying a word as they explained the contest.

Mae also never thought she'd be asking Bubba for a second favor, but then again, she never thought she'd ride his bike and pull her sister in his wagon all the way to the hospital. Or that he would ride the entire way beside her. This was a summer full of *nevers* turned into *possibles*. And just maybe Bubba would agree to be Miss Fannie's assistant.

Bubba stood and wiped the sweat that pooled above his lip. "Nobody knows I can bake, and I'd like to keep it that way," he said. "I sorta got a reputation for being a—um—" He couldn't find the word.

"A bully?" Jimmy Mac found it for him.

Bubba nodded. "Yeah, and if people knew I liked to bake cookies and cakes, well, they wouldn't take me serious."

"Bubba," Mae stood beside him. "Maybe you could give them a reason to finally see you different."

Bubba raised his eyebrows. "Such as?"

Mae wondered if he was testing her. "People would take you serious because you make seriously good cakes and cookies," she said.

Jimmy Mac nodded and gave Mae a look like she was saying all the right words. She could always make a good argument, but this was one of her best. And it was for her once sworn enemy.

The trailer door opened, and sunlight streamed in, almost blinding Mae and Jimmy Mac.

"I didn't know we had company," Beecher said, stepping out of his lace-less tennis shoes.

A smell floated through the trailer. It was like the air conditioner had just kicked on, and a skunk was trapped inside it.

Bubba picked up one of the shoes and threw it at Beecher. "You know Mama don't let us bring our shoes inside." Beecher hunted for the shoe and tossed them both out the door. He sat on the couch beside Jimmy Mac.

Mae started where she left off. "Plus, think about all she's taught you." She looked at Bubba. She couldn't read his face. She needed to crank it up. "Miss Fannie's been your only friend."

"*I'm* Bubba's friend," Beecher interrupted.

Mae gave Beecher an annoyed look. "You're family. It don't count." She turned back to Bubba. "Miss Fannie spends time with you because she cares about you. And now she needs you."

Jimmy Mac stood and slapped Bubba's back, his hand sliding on Bubba's sweat-drenched shirt. He wiped his hand on his jeans. "It's time to fish or cut bait," Jimmy Mac said.

"Yeah, you gotta poop or get off the pot," Beecher added. "What are we talking about?"

Mae was tired of telling the story, so Jimmy Mac took a turn. When he was done, Beecher asked, "You mean all this time I could've been eating desserts every day?"

Bubba grinned and said, "Okay, I'm in."

CHAPTER TWENTY

Early the next morning, Miss Fannie called Mae's mama. Mae listened from the hall as her mama tried to convince Miss Fannie to enter the bake sale.

As soon as she said goodbye, Mae raced into the kitchen. "What'd she say?"

"The Gilbert brothers called her," she answered, putting the phone down. "And as soon as they said there'd be a crowd and a camera, Fannie said, 'No way, no how.'"

Mae's shoulders slumped. "Why'd they have to say that part? Right up front?"

Her mama rinsed a cereal bowl. "She said Davis Hampton called her next."

Mae perked up.

"Fannie said he was giving her a gift." Mae's mama turned the bowl over on the strainer.

"What kind of gift?" Mae asked, bending over the sink to read her mama's expression.

She washed a glass. "Fannie didn't say." Her mama turned to Mae and smiled big. "Just that it was enough to help her decide she should do it."

Mae hugged her mama tight. *Davis came through,* Mae thought.

Mae's mama told her the Gilbert brothers had explained the rules to Miss Fannie. "One of them said the rules were simple, but Fannie said, 'There ain't nothing simple when it comes to Alice Weatherall and her peaches!'"

Basically, The Donut Hole Bake Sale would go like this: The brothers would work on enough of The Donut Hole to install two industrial style ovens, new countertops, one giant-sized refrigerator, and one super-sized pantry stocked with baking essentials like cookie sheets, pans, mixers, and the like. According to Miss Fannie, most of the work was already done. Both ladies would be given $200 each for groceries, and they would bring in the groceries and receipts the night before the bake sale.

Each baker, along with an assistant, would be given two hours to bake. Then, each would have a team of three helpers to sell the items on the sidewalk in front of the shop. At the end of those two hours, whoever had sold the most would win The Donut Hole.

Mae shook her head. "She ain't got a chance."

Her daddy pushed Shelby in from the living room. "What's with gloomy Gladys?" he asked.

Mae looked at her daddy. "Miss Fannie's gonna lose 'cause Mr. Weatherall will buy all of his wife's stuff."

Mae's mama put her arm around her. "They took care of that. Only three items per customer are allowed."

Mae smiled, then drooped her shoulders again.

"What now?" her daddy asked. He gave Shelby a spoonful of yogurt. Shelby scrunched up her nose, and Mae saw that it was peach flavor instead of her usual favorite.

Mae pulled out a chair from the table and plopped down. "They'll get all their relatives to come in from out of town to buy everything."

"They thought of that too," her mama said. "A customer will also have to show identification, proving they're from Jessup."

"Makes sense. Once the winner has the bakery up and running as their own, it'll be townsfolk who will shop there, not once-in-a-lifetime-visitors, like—oh, I don't know—Alice's brother," her daddy said.

Mae's mama shook her head.

Her daddy gave Shelby another spoonful, but she pushed it out with her tongue.

"But I heard he'd gained thirty pounds and gone bald," he said, grinning. "So Sam's welcome any time."

Mae's mama smacked him with a dish towel.

———

Mae woke up with a stomach full of hummingbirds the next morning. She and her mama were meeting Miss Fannie and Bubba in the Piggly Wiggly parking lot that afternoon to give them a good-luck gift.

They pulled into a parking space at four on the dot and spotted Miss Fannie on the Piggly Wiggly bench with Bubba and Beecher on either side.

Mae grabbed the car door handle and felt a pang of panic. "What if Miss Fannie doesn't win?" She gave her mama a worried look. "What if I got her all excited for nothing?"

Mae's mama took her hand. "Are you kidding me? This is the biggest thing to hit Jessup in a long time. Win or lose, you've been a part of it." She squeezed Mae's hand tighter. "You brought Fannie some hope."

Mae's heart tingled. Maybe the hope she'd been looking for could only be found once you gave it away. She tucked the thought in the back of her brain until she could lawn-chair it with the preacher.

They finally got out of the car and walked toward Miss Fannie and the boys. Her mama carried two blue gift bags with yellow tissue paper sticking out. They got close, and her mama stopped dead in her tracks. "Fannie! Where'd you get your smile?" Mae's mama asked.

Miss Fannie smiled big, showing a full set of teeth. "You like 'em? Davis got 'em for me." She turned her head, smiling so that everyone in a five-mile radius could see her dentures.

Miss Fannie explained Davis had put away some of his bonus money from the Braves. "He said he'd been saving it for just the right purchase," Miss Fannie said. She looked like she might start crying, and Bubba gave a here-we-go-again kind of look. "Davis said if I joined the bake sale for him, he'd get new teeth for me." Miss Fannie started full-on bawling.

Mae's mama hugged her. "You look beautiful," she said.

Miss Fannie wiped her eyes with her hand. "What you got there?" she asked, looking at the bags.

Mae's mama handed Miss Fannie one of the gifts. "It's not near as good as what Davis gave you," Mae said, handing the other bag to Bubba.

Miss Fannie took out the tissue paper and threw it over her shoulder. She pulled out an apron and held it in front of her.

"Now you'll look like professional bakers," Mae said.

Bubba took his out and looked at it. Mae's mama had gotten the aprons from Mr. Smith. They were bright yellow and on the front said:

SMITH'S HARDWARE

WHERE THERE'S A BOLT FOR EVERY NUT!

But right below, Mae's mom had used fabric paint and written:

MISS FANNIE AND BUBBA'S GOODIES BAKED GREAT!

Beecher laughed. Everybody looked at him, and he got the message: there would be no teasing Bubba on account of he was wearing an apron.

"We love them, don't we, Bubba?" Miss Fannie said, elbowing Bubba.

"Thanks, Mrs. Moore," he said. Miss Fannie jabbed him harder. "And Mae," he added.

Mae's mama wrapped the apron strings behind Bubba's back. "Who have you decided on to help sell your goods?" Mae's mama asked Miss Fannie as she tied Bubba's apron.

"Well, seeing how this is all Mae Ellen's idea, I thought I'd let her pick," Miss Fannie said.

Beecher's eyes widened. Mae couldn't decide if it was because he wanted to be asked or because he was afraid he might get asked. She had a fifty-fifty chance of making his day.

"I've been chewing on that," Mae said. "Of course, there's me." Everyone nodded or "uh-hum'ed." "I've been going back and forth between Jimmy Mac and Beecher here," she said, pointing to Beecher. He took in a big breath. "And I've decided even though he can be clumsy at times, Jimmy Mac is the logical choice."

Beecher let out a bunch of air. "Whew, that was close," he said. "I couldn't take the pressure." His cousin gave him a confused look. "Of Miss Fannie getting The Donut Hole resting on my shoulders," he said, looking at Bubba.

"Your shoulders?" Bubba punched his cousin. "I'm the one doing the baking with her." He turned pale and looked sick.

"Bubba, don't you worry none," Miss Fannie said, patting his back. "We got this."

Mae was proud of Miss Fannie's confidence—until she saw her give Mae's mama a what-have-I-gotten-myself-into look.

Mae needed to get things back on track. "And our ace in the hole—what's gonna make sure Miss Fannie sells the most—is a bona fide celebrity," Mae announced.

"Who?" her mama asked.

Mae saw the red truck stop at the traffic light on Main Street. "There's our secret weapon," Mae said, waving her arms. "Davis!" she yelled, trying to get his attention so that he'd pull into the parking lot.

He looked straight ahead. Mae walked to the edge of the street, just yards from the intersection. "Davis!" she yelled louder. *Why isn't he looking at me?* she wondered. She yelled again. Nothing.

She marched up to his truck. "Mae Ellen Moore!" her mama hollered. "Get out of the street!"

Mae stared at him. "Dang it, Davis. What is your problem?" she asked, her hands on her hips.

"Light's about to turn green," Davis said, pointing ahead.

"Then pull over," she demanded, clenching her teeth.

"I'm running late," he said. Mae wasn't budging. The light turned green, and Davis looked in his rearview mirror. There were two cars behind him. Davis sighed loudly and pulled over.

Mae moved to the sidewalk, where she was safe from oncoming traffic. She crossed her arms and reclenched her jaw. How could he get Miss Fannie her teeth one day, then ignore her the next? *Why can't he stay the Davis who took me to Miss Fannie's trailer that day?* she wondered.

She figured she needed to simmer down if she had any hope of getting him to help with the bake sale. "That was nice, what you did for Miss Fannie," she said.

"It was nothing," he said, thumping the steering wheel. Davis refused to look at Mae.

"Tomorrow's the big day," she said, faking a smile.

"Uh-huh," he said. "It sure is."

"So, we're gonna need your help selling—" Mae started.

Davis turned to her, his nostrils flaring. "I'm busy tomorrow," he said. "I'm done with the community service."

Mae squinted her eyes hard and wrinkled her nose. "Community service?" she said. "That's what we are to you?" Her neck and face turned red.

"Look, I put in sixty-two hours hauling crap out of that stinking trailer park. Two more than the judge ordered," he said, his voice getting louder. "Then carting you around to get your cake, taking Miss Fannie to get—"

"What?" Mae said. Her fists balled up beside her legs.

"I'm not about to sell brownies so the entire town can gawk at me." Davis put his truck in reverse. "I don't have any more time to spend on you—" he pointed to her mama and friends standing in front of the Piggly Wiggly "—or them."

Davis backed up. "Or this stupid town." He peeled off.

Mae watched his truck drive off until she couldn't see it anymore. For a second, she thought she might cry, but she took a big breath. *I am not wasting any tears on that lowdown, no-good Davis Hampton,* she thought. *If he doesn't want to be a part of the biggest thing to hit Jessup, it's fine by me.*

Mae turned around. Her mama and Miss Fannie were staring at her. Bubba's and Beecher's mouths were wide open. She hoped they hadn't heard what was said, especially the community service part, but by the looks of things, they had.

"So we won't have a celebrity selling Miss Fannie's baked goods, drawing attention to her table, helping her out-sell the competition. So what?" Mae mumbled to herself as she marched back to them.

"Young lady, what was that all about?" her mama shouted. "We do not walk in the middle of the street." Her mama remembered it wasn't just her and Mae, so she lowered her voice. "And we certainly do not yell at passing motorists. Especially ones who have been in jail."

"He's not coming tomorrow, is he?" Beecher asked.

Mae straightened up, remembering she was the one who had started this whole ball rolling in the first place. She wasn't about to let one setback get in the way. "Good news." Mae pointed to Beecher. "You're back in."

Beecher gulped. "I was afraid of that."

Miss Fannie told the boys it was time to ride home and rest up so they could "bake and sell like nobody's business tomorrow." They watched until Beecher and Bubba got down the street.

"I coulda told you Davis wouldn't be available," Miss Fannie said. She looked at Mae's mama, then at Mae, like she had a secret. "He doesn't want anyone to know, but there's a scout coming into town tomorrow. He's gonna watch him throw."

Mae looked at her sneakers. She felt her body unwind. "Pitch," she mumbled. She looked up at Miss Fannie. "Sounds like he got his second chance."

Miss Fannie nodded. "He can't help that his comes the same day as mine." Miss Fannie smiled. Out of habit she raised her hand to cover her teeth, then remembered she didn't have to anymore.

Mae thought back to the day Davis seemed different—rude even—at the grocery store when she first told him about The Donut Hole. And at the hospital, he kept looking at his watch like he had to be somewhere. It was probably the field so that he could practice. And now, today. "Why didn't he just say that?" she asked.

"I think he's afraid to get everyone's hopes up again," Miss Fannie said. "Especially his own."

Part of Mae was glad for Davis. She wanted him to make a comeback. But part of her wondered if the only reason he'd been nice in the first place was like he'd said—community service. They were just a part of the punishment the judge had given him. And now that he had put in his time, he was done.

CHAPTER
TWENTY-ONE

Miss Fannie's check-in time at The Donut Hole was 4:45 p.m. that afternoon. Mae and her mama helped Miss Fannie take her groceries in. The executive producer for *Flip This Flop* was also there to go over each item and the Piggly Wiggly receipt.

Miss Fannie, Mae, and her mama looked around the almost-new Donut Hole. Mae watched as Miss Fannie inspected the ovens and refrigerator. She looked at the pantry like it was Christmas morning.

As they headed out the door, Savanna and Mrs. Weatherall walked in. Savanna's daddy pulled their groceries in a wagon behind them. It wasn't loaded with Piggly Wiggly groceries— theirs was in bags from some store Mae had never heard of. *Big mistake,* Mae thought. *Can't buy near as much stuff at the fancy stores.*

"Hello, Alice," Mae's mama said. Savanna and Mae wrinkled their noses at each other.

"Leigh Ann. Fannie," Mrs. Weatherall said. Her purse hung at her elbow, and she clutched her sunglasses in her hand.

Savanna's daddy smiled at them. "Fannie, I've been meaning to stop by the store to tell you—those cupcakes you made for my birthday were dee-lish." He caught his wife's eye and gave a shrug. "Both of you ladies are winners in my book," he said. He looked to his wife for approval, but she wasn't giving any.

"I'm glad you liked them," Miss Fannie said. Mr. and Mrs. Weatherall looked at Miss Fannie like they noticed something different about her but couldn't figure out what it was.

The place was filled with an awkward silence until the *Flip This Flop* producer motioned for the Weatheralls to get checked in at the counter.

The Donut Hole door shut behind them, leaving Miss Fannie, Mae, and her mama standing on the sidewalk. "Well, that's that," Miss Fannie said nervously.

"Yes, it is," Mae's mama said.

"There's nothing to do but pray and get a good night's sleep," Miss Fannie said.

———

As soon as they got home from taking Miss Fannie to Happy Acres, Mae hopped on her bike. If she hustled, she could make it to drive-thru prayer before Preacher Floyd folded up his lawn chair.

Twenty minutes later she sat across from him, sipping a bottled water. She caught him up to speed on Shelby and her daddy's recoveries, the bake sale's official rules, and Davis's meeting with the scout. If he already knew about the Major League Baseball scout coming to town, he didn't let on.

"What I don't get is why his big day has to fall on the same day as Miss Fannie's," she said.

The preacher took a drink of water. "The Lord works in mysterious ways."

Mae frowned. That seemed to be his answer when he didn't have an answer.

"It's just—I had it all worked out." Mae looked at the ground. "Miss Fannie has a bigger chance of winning if Davis is there." She looked at the preacher. "His comeback tryout wasn't part of the plan."

The preacher removed his hat. He took a hankie from his back pocket and wiped the sweat from his forehead. "Part of *your* plan," he said.

"That's what I said."

He tilted his head and looked at her.

"Oh," Mae said. "Maybe my plan isn't the only plan?"

Preacher Floyd smiled. "Or the best plan."

Mae sat back in her chair. She thought about Shelby, how she had held her sister on the front porch, telling her she was sorry. Hoping and praying she'd be all right. Carting her to the hospital in Bubba's wagon. She certainly hadn't planned any of that.

And then her other plan—the one where she didn't have a sister. Mae sighed. Thank goodness she didn't get her ninth birthday wish. Instead, she got something else: forgiveness for not accepting the perfect sister she'd been given.

"So what you're saying is—" Mae stopped. Her eyes brimmed with tears. She realized she'd also been given a chance to prove to Shelby—and perhaps herself—that she loved Shelby exactly the way she was. All of her.

"It takes faith," the preacher said.

"Faith," Mae repeated. She finally understood. She had to believe God knew exactly what He was doing when He made her family. It wasn't random or a matter of good luck or bad luck. It was planned.

Then she remembered the preacher's family and the sadness he must carry. "I'm sorry about your son," she said.

The preacher looked at her. "Thank you, Mae Ellen. Matthew was a good boy. Always helping others. Loving them no matter what." He smiled. "His mother and I miss him every day. But we believe God's ways are better than ours. Even when we don't understand those ways."

Mae nodded.

"'Faith, hope, and love,'" the preacher reminded her. "'And the greatest of these—'"

"'Is love,'" they said together.

CHAPTER TWENTY-TWO

Things were hopping at The Donut Hole the morning of the bake sale. The Gilbert brothers had set up tables and chairs for the audience to watch the baking. After, everyone would move outside for the actual selling portion of the competition.

Even though her part wasn't for a couple of hours, Mae wanted to watch the two-hour baking portion. Mae's daddy and Shelby dropped her off on the way to take Mae's mama to her shift at the grocery store. With vehicles parked everywhere, Mae's daddy had to pull sideways behind the *Flip This Flop* van.

They watched a man carry a huge camera into the shop. Mae and her mama looked at each other. *She's not one to seek the limelight,* Mae remembered Davis saying. Mae's mama must have known what her daughter was thinking because she said, "Fannie will be fine."

Jimmy Mac and his mama walked by. "Twila looks good," her mama said. "I haven't seen her in ages."

Mae smiled to see Jimmy Mac's mama out in public. She knew it gave her best friend hope that his mama would be okay. "Maybe Mrs. Twila should've been Miss Fannie's assistant," Mae said. "She's a darn good lunch lady."

Jimmy Mac tripped over a cable snaking into The Donut Hole. If his mama hadn't grabbed his arm, he would've face-planted on the sidewalk. "Never mind. She's got her hands full trying to keep Jimmy Mac alive."

Mae's mama laughed. "I'll take my lunch break early and come over to buy my share of cookies," she said.

"Shelby Grace and I'll be back later too," her daddy said.

Mae nodded. It'd be too long a day for Shelby to be at the shop. Plus, Miss Fannie needed everybody they knew to be there starting at ten o'clock. With their wallets open.

"All right, you need to skedaddle," her daddy said. "Sitting behind this van is bringing back memories." Her daddy looked at Mae in his rearview mirror. "And they're not good ones."

He tried to sound serious, but Mae saw his grin. Ever since the Gilbert Brothers had walked into the hospital room, she'd been thinking about how good things could sometimes come from bad things. The train wreck was a perfect example. But there were lots of others.

"I'm sure a couple of cookies will take my mind off all this itching." Her daddy knocked on his boot. It was on his left foot, so he could still drive, but he'd said it itched like a sock full of sand fleas. "Tell Fannie good luck for us," he said.

The Donut Hole was packed with people sitting at tables and other folks standing along the walls. Mae spotted an empty chair next to Jimmy Mac, his mama, and Beecher. A sign stood on the nearby tabletop: "Fannie Higgins's Team."

Mrs. Twila gave Mae a hug. "Hey, girl," she said. "We've got a front-row seat."

Mae nodded. She looked to the right half of the shop where Miss Fannie and Bubba were talking with Jace Gilbert. Then her eyes shifted to the left side where Mrs. Weatherall and Savanna were talking with Cam Gilbert. "They're going over last-minute rules," Jimmy Mac said.

Mae looked for the Weatherall Team table. She found Mr. Weatherall, Savanna's grandparents, and her uncle, Sam Meredith—who looked just like his sister with a full head of hair—sitting together. She noticed the big clock that hung on the wall. It read 7:55 a.m. She swallowed hard.

The Gilbert brothers moved to the center of the shop. Two cameras got in position in front of them; one pointed at the audience and another at the bakers.

"Hi, everybody," Jace said. "We'd like to welcome you to the first-ever bake sale on *Flip This Flop!*"

Mae glanced around as everyone clapped. She couldn't get over how the contest had brought everybody out. Leaning on the side wall was Mrs. Britt, her fifth-grade teacher, and Sue from the beauty parlor. Dr. Heery and his wife were sitting at the back table. Heck, almost the whole town was there or would be by the time things got exciting on the sidewalk.

Mae looked at the front door—he wasn't coming. Davis wasn't there now, and he wouldn't be later. His community service was over. The words still stung.

Cam explained the rules to the audience and said clips of what happened today would play in the first of the "Small-Town Renovations" episodes of *Flip This Flop*. Mrs. Twila folded down Jimmy Mac's shirt collar. He was dressed in his pressed Sunday clothes—more assurance that his prayer for his mama was getting answered.

"Let's meet our two contestants and their assistants before the baking begins," Jace said. "Give it up for Alice Weatherall and her assistant, her eleven-year-old daughter, Savanna."

People clapped. *Figures they'd be first,* Mae thought. She patted her leg instead of clapping both hands. Savanna and her mother wore matching pink aprons, monogrammed with their initials. Mae rolled her eyes when she read what was embroidered on the center of their aprons: "Sweeter than a Georgia Peach."

Savanna spotted Mae at the Team Miss Fannie table. She gave a smile that said, "We are so gonna beat you." Mae noticed something on Savanna's teeth. She looked harder. It was a red lipstick stain. Mae giggled to herself, thinking about how she'd be sure to point that out to the Riverside Middle School student body when the show aired.

Then she thought again, kinder thoughts this time. Savanna was representing Jessup too. Mae rubbed her finger over her own top front teeth, but Savanna was too busy staring at Jimmy Mac.

Mae whispered to him, "You might wanna tell your girl-friend she has lipstick on her teeth."

"For the hundredth time, she's not my girlfriend," he whispered back. He pointed to his teeth, though. Savanna finally got the hint and rubbed the red stain off with her tongue.

"And let's give a warm welcome to Fannie Higgins and her assistant, Bubba Duncan," Cam announced. Everyone clapped, and Mae watched Miss Fannie. She reminded Mae of Dorothy arriving in Oz. Miss Fannie looked at the lights, which were mounted on huge metal rods hanging from the ceiling, the padded microphone dangling above their heads, and the cameras.

Instead of the usual hairnet she wore behind the Piggly Wiggly bakery counter, Miss Fannie held back her hair with a fancy red scarf. It had specks of yellow in it that matched the apron from Smith's Hardware. Miss Fannie scanned the audience until she found her friends, then she smiled big, showing off her new teeth.

Bubba had cleaned up and washed and combed his blond curls. He looked more nervous than a long-tailed cat in a room full of rocking chairs. He shifted his weight from one foot to the other. Mae wondered if she should have been more worried about him than Miss Fannie all along. Mae glanced back and forth between the two of them. *Pretend you're baking in Miss Fannie's trailer,* she thought.

"It's time to get down to baking business," Jace said. "Our bakers will have exactly two hours to bake everything they'll sell later."

Cam Gilbert looked at his watch, and Miss Fannie grabbed Bubba's hand. "Five, four, three, two, one. Bake!" Cam yelled.

The bakers and their assistants rushed to the pantry and refrigerator and loaded their arms with sugar, flour, eggs, and the other ingredients they'd bought the night before.

Both Miss Fannie and Mrs. Weatherall had their own oven, sink, and countertop, but the space was tiny and confined. Savanna and her mother kept bumping into each other, knocking butts once. Mae watched Miss Fannie and Bubba. Both were nervous, but they moved well together. Baking in Miss Fannie's cramped Happy Acres kitchen was good practice for the tight space they were baking in now.

Once things were underway, the audience talked and moved around to different tables, but Mae stayed glued to her seat, watching Miss Fannie and Bubba. Miss Fannie worked the stand-up mixer with one hand and fanned herself with a spatula with the other. Their heads were almost touching as Bubba gradually pushed the dry ingredients into the mixer's bowl with his fingertips.

Mae watched Savanna and her mama. Both were furiously peeling and slicing peaches. Butter crackled in a cast-iron skillet on the stove in front of them. *I like peach cobbler as much as anyone, but is that all they're gonna make?* Mae wondered.

She shifted her eyes back to the other side. Beads of sweat pooled above Bubba's top lip as he and Miss Fannie used ice cream scoops to drop cookie batter onto five huge trays.

Cameras moved around the kitchen's two stations, in between the bakers and their creations. When Savanna knew she was being filmed, she'd toss her long hair back and smile big. Bubba gave a crooked grin and looked like he might puke whenever the camera pointed in his direction. Miss Fannie kept her head and eyes focused on her cookie sheets.

Jace tried to make small talk with Miss Fannie and Bubba. "So what all you got in these cookies of yours, Miss Fannie?" He reached in with a spoon and scraped the side of the bowl. He ate the cookie dough and licked the back of the spoon.

Miss Fannie darted her eyes up at him, then quickly looked back at her trays lined with parchment paper. Cam squeezed between Miss Fannie and Bubba. "Bubba, tell us about your Triple Cs." Bubba opened his mouth, then shut it as soon as Miss Fannie gave him a look.

"Fannie, do you use milk chocolate or semi-chocolate chips in your recipe?" Cam tried again.

Jimmy Mac tapped Mae's elbow, then leaned in. "How come she won't talk?" Mae nervously drummed the tabletop with her fingers.

"Fannie?" Cam said.

Miss Fannie glanced at Bubba. He had turned as white as rice, and Mae worried he might faint. "Can't tell you," Miss Fannie said.

"Oh, come on," he insisted.

Miss Fannie put her hands on her hips. "I said I can't say."

"Uh-oh," Mae whispered. Miss Fannie's short fuse was showing.

Once at the Piggly Wiggly, Mae had witnessed a customer telling Miss Fannie she'd put too many chopped pecans in the brownies. Miss Fannie had taken off her apron, held it over the bakery counter, and said, "If you think you know more about baking than me, c'mon over." The man ended up buying all the brownies in the case and two dozen cupcakes. Mae's mama had told Mae he was afraid Miss Fannie might ban him from the bakery.

"It's a family secret," Bubba said, deciding he'd better get involved.

Mae held her breath. *Don't let this be a deal breaker,* she thought.

"Smart business move, Fannie," Cam said. "If you gave the recipe away, anybody could make them."

Mae relaxed, relieved Fannie didn't blow a gasket.

Then she looked at the Weatherall side of the Donut Hole. Savanna handed Jace a peach, and he took a bite. Peach juice ran down his chin. They looked chummy, and Mae didn't like it one bit.

"They said the winner would be the one who sold the most," Mae said to Jimmy Mac. "But what if it's who they *like* the most?"

"Folks like Miss Fannie and Bubba," Beecher said.

Mae and Jimmy Mac looked at each other, then at Beecher. "Well, folks do like Miss Fannie," Beecher said.

"We'll have to sell with all we got," Jimmy Mac said. "Like our lives depend on it."

Like her life *depended on it*, Mae thought. That's exactly why they needed Davis Hampton. He was all part of Mae's plan—the one she had before he ruined it. She started to steam up again until she remembered God had His own plans. Mae let out a deep breath, and her face softened.

Jace announced there was exactly one hour left in the baking portion of the competition. Miss Fannie and Bubba spent the remaining time making red velvet cupcakes with cream cheese icing and blond brownies. Alice and Savanna Weatherall finished up their cobblers, then made peanut butter bars with a layer of peach preserves in the middle.

Fannie pulled out the last of their goodies from the oven as Cam counted down again. "Five, four, three, two, one. Stop baking!" he hollered.

Miss Fannie and Bubba looked plum wore out. Bubba wiped the sweat from his forehead with his arm.

Now it was time for Mae to kick it into gear. She, Jimmy Mac, and Beecher set up a thirty-foot table on their side of the sidewalk in front of The Donut Hole. Miss Fannie had bought a pretty tablecloth with yellow and orange gerbera daisies on it with part of the *Flip This Flop* money. Jimmy Mac and Beecher each took an end and covered the table, then Mae smoothed it down with her hands.

Miss Fannie and Bubba walked out carrying baskets full of goodies and a tray of cupcakes. They'd cut the brownies into 3-by-3-inch squares and packaged two cookies to a baggie. Bubba had scooped the leftover cupcake icing onto plastic spoons and placed them in baggies, too, just like the ones Miss Fannie gave Shelby. Miss Fannie and Bubba had done their part, and now it was up to the sales team and the customers.

All items were priced at fifty cents or a dollar. But unlike regular bake sales, they couldn't take any donations. Producers from *Flip This Flop* stood at each table to check IDs, making sure all the buyers were from Jessup and that the other rules were followed. The Jace brothers had said they wanted the best baker to win. Once they turned the bakery over to the winner, she'd have to make it on her own.

Beecher, Jimmy Mac, and Mae laid the items out, leaving what wouldn't fit in baskets behind the table. Mae stepped back, admiring their display. Then she looked at Savanna and her mama's table.

The Weatheralls had scooped their peach cobbler into little cups with tiny spoons attached. Then they'd set each one in a clear box with a ribbon tied around it. The peanut butter bars were wrapped in pink and green tissue paper, then placed in bags that looked like mini purses.

"We're sunk," Mae muttered under her breath.

"What's wrong?" Beecher asked. Mae pointed to the competition. He looked at Savanna's table with all its fancy packaging, then at the Piggly Wiggly brand baggies lined up on theirs.

"It don't matter how they look, only how they taste, remember?" Jimmy Mac said. Mae gave him a look like he had two heads. Then she remembered that's what she had said the day Davis agreed to talk Miss Fannie into the bake sale. *Davis.* He was her secret weapon. His celebrity status could have helped move the goods. But he wasn't coming.

Hey, wait a minute, Mae thought. She walked over to Miss Fannie, who was standing behind the table and smiling nervously at the customers looking at her cookies. "I think there's been some cheatin'," Mae whispered to Miss Fannie.

Miss Fannie leaned closer to Mae. "How so?" she asked.

"There's no way Mrs. Weatherall could have bought fancy packaging and all her baking ingredients for $200," Mae said. "She spent some of her own money," Mae said.

Mae looked at the Weatherall table. It was surrounded by customers "oohing" and "aahing" over her stuff. Only Dr. Heery, his wife, and a few folks from Miss Fannie's church were buying something from Beecher. She looked at their money drawer. Eight one-dollar bills and a few quarters. It wasn't going to get Miss Fannie her bakery.

"The peaches!" Mae shouted.

CHAPTER TWENTY-THREE

M iss Fannie grabbed Mae's hand. "Hush, girl."

"But they got those for free—straight from their own trees. They had an unfair advantage," Mae said. "I'm telling Jace."

"No, you're not," Miss Fannie said. "I don't wanna win because Alice Weatherall got disqualified. I wanna win because folks think what I got is better." Miss Fannie let go of Mae's hand. "And they'd come to my bakery." She dabbed at her eyes. "If I had one."

"What you got *is* better," Mae said. "And we're gonna do everything we can to get you your bakery." She took a big breath. "Miss Fannie's famous Triple Cs over here!" Mae shouted. "Loaded with chocolatey—" she couldn't come up with the right words "—ooey, gooey chocolate." Mae bopped herself in the forehead. *That won't sell squat,* she thought.

"Give me the works," Preacher Floyd said, stepping up to the table. He showed his driver's license to the lady producer.

Mae smiled. "This here's Preacher Floyd Foster." The producer nodded. "He's about the smartest person I know," Mae said as she took his three dollars. "And you'll notice he's at Miss Fannie's table."

"Well, to be fair, Wanda's over at Alice's table buying peach cobbler." The preacher leaned over the table. "But I know for a fact she's only got a dollar on her," he said, winking at Mae.

Mae's mama walked from the grocery store and got in line to buy something. Her daddy came down the sidewalk with his big boot on and pushed Shelby's wheelchair right next to Mae. While her daddy and mama each bought their maximum allowance of sweets, Bubba approached Shelby.

Mae's heart stopped. And then started again when he offered a spoonful of icing to her sister. "Miss Fannie says you like these," Bubba said softly. Shelby looked up at Bubba and clapped.

Mae saw a gentleness in Bubba's eyes she hadn't ever noticed before. "Miss Fannie's cream cheese and butter icing is her favorite," she said. Mae took the plastic spoon out of the baggie for Shelby. "Thanks, Bubba."

Mae's mama put her arm around him. "That was sweet, Bubba," she said. He blushed, then looked at his shoes. "We should go say hello to Sam," Mae's mama said so that everyone would stop staring at Bubba.

"Good idea," her daddy said. "Distract him from selling his sister's stuff."

Mae's mama shook her head. "C'mon," she said.

In between customers, Mae watched her parents talk with Savanna's uncle. She wondered if things might get ugly between her daddy and her mama's once-upon-a-time boyfriend. She was sure her daddy could take Sam Meredith if they went to scuffling. And if they did, she hoped one of them would turn over the Weatherall table and spill all their merchandise in the process.

But all they did was talk. When Mae saw her mama and Sam hug, she thought it might start something, but then her daddy and Sam shook hands. *It's weird how once enemies can become friends,* Mae thought. She looked at Bubba leaning on the wall outside of The Donut Hole, hands in his pockets. *Really weird.*

They had sold for one solid hour, and it was time to see where things stood money-wise. Both producers had taken the money drawers and were counting up the cash.

Cam and Jace stood in front of the tables as the cameras got in position. "We're at the halfway mark, and I bet everyone's wondering which baker has sold the most so far," Cam said. Jace handed him a piece of paper with the totals on it.

Miss Fannie got up from the metal folding chair by her table and stood next to Bubba.

"With one hour left," Cam said, "the Weatherall Team has sold one hundred and fifty-six dollars and fifty cents worth of cobbler and peanut butter bars."

People clapped. Mae looked at Bubba. He had his eyes closed and fingers crossed under his chin.

"And the Higgins Team—"

Mae held her breath.

"—has sold one hundred and thirteen dollars' worth of baked goods," Cam announced.

Savanna and her mama hugged and jumped up and down.

Mae sighed. *If only Davis were here.* Mae tried to see how Miss Fannie took the news, but she couldn't get a good look on account of Mr. Adams, the Piggly Wiggly manager, standing in front of Miss Fannie.

"How's it going, Fannie?" he asked.

"Well, as you might've heard, we're coming up a bit short," Miss Fannie answered.

"Your cookies have always been my favorite, but I like anything you bake." Mr. Adams handed Jimmy Mac some money and took one of each item for sale. "Good luck, Fannie," Mr. Adams said, walking back to work. Fannie smiled the biggest Mae'd ever seen.

"We've got to drum up more business," Jimmy Mac said. "I'm going to the hardware store to see if I can talk people into coming by." Mae nodded, and Jimmy Mac took off down the street.

Beecher put out the rest of the baked goods. What was on the table was all that was left to sell. Mae craned her neck to see Savanna's table. They didn't have as much stuff. Either they hadn't baked as much to begin with, or they'd already sold most of what they had.

Three kids from the elementary school walked up to Miss Fannie's table. Each handed over fifty cents. "They're giving out free sodas at the Piggly Wiggly to anybody who buys something from Miss Fannie," one of the kids said. Mae looked at the *Flip This Flop* producer, wondering if a thrown-in freebie was legal. The producer shrugged her shoulders like it was okay. Then Mae saw her turn her head and take a bite of a cookie.

After a few more grocery shoppers and two men Jimmy Mac had escorted down from the hardware store left, things got quiet. So quiet, Mae, Jimmy Mac, Bubba, and Beecher sat on the curb. Miss Fannie stayed in her metal chair, fanning herself with the skirt of her apron.

"We only got twenty minutes left," Beecher said, glancing at his watch. "Think we'll—I mean—Miss Fannie will win?"

"She's got to," Bubba said. "I ain't worked so hard or wanted something so much in my whole life."

Mae saw the two *Flip This Flop* producers talking. She elbowed Jimmy Mac. "Look," she said. "They know who's ahead."

They all turned around. "How can you tell?" Beecher asked.

The producer who had been at Miss Fannie's table had her eyes down. She looked disappointed. "That's how," Mae said, pointing at her.

"It's not fair," Beecher said. "We worked real hard."

"We *did* work!" Mae was about to say Davis hadn't worked at all and how he could've been—should've been—there, but she realized whining wouldn't help the situation. "Sometimes it ain't enough." She slapped her legs and stood. "Let's make a good showing all the way to the end. For Miss Fannie."

The boys slowly rose, then turned toward the sound of a school bus coming up the street.

"What's it doing here?" Bubba asked. "School don't start for two more weeks."

Mae looked through the front window of the bus. The Tigers' baseball coach was driving. The bus stopped in front of them, and the door folded open. "Right this way, folks," Davis said, hopping off the steps. He pointed to Miss Fannie's table.

Davis looked at Mae. "We made a sweep through Happy Acres," he said.

Miss Fannie hugged each of her neighbors as they approached her table.

"Things happened so fast there at the end," Davis said, "and Miss Fannie didn't have time to tell her neighbors about the contest."

Nothing came out of Mae's mouth even though it was wide open.

"Miss Fannie's given away dozens of cookies to her neighbors over the years," Davis said. "They wanted to return the favor." He looked at the goods on the table. "Triple Cs? I'd trade my right arm for one of Miss Fannie's cookies." Miss Fannie gave Davis a bear hug, and she would've lifted him off the ground if she weren't so tired from all her baking.

"Miss Fannie used to send the Tigers a box of sweets before each game, didn't you?" Davis shouted. "That's how we won State."

A swarm of customers surrounded Miss Fannie's table. Mayor Howard reached out to shake Davis's hand. "That was some game," he said.

Mae turned to Beecher. "This means I'm out, right?" he asked.

Mae shrugged. "Sorry."

Beecher reached inside his shorts' pocket and took out two quarters. "Finally," he said, handing Jimmy Mac the money. Beecher picked up a baggie of cookies, pulled one out, and took a bite. "She's got to win," he said through a mouthful of chocolate.

Mae wanted to ask Davis why he'd changed his mind. *The tryout must've been earlier this morning,* Mae thought. *He tried out and then he got to feeling guilty. That's why he's here now.* Or maybe he'd miscounted and was short two hours on his community service. He was made to come! Mae's heart started to harden.

People crowded around Davis, asking about that last game and what it was like to play for the Braves. Nobody mentioned him getting fired or his jail time. In between answering questions he'd say, "What'll it be? Triple Cs, cupcakes, or brownies?" He was making sure to push the merchandise. "Or how about one of these delicious icing spoons?" he added. "Where have these been all my life?" he asked, licking the back of his spoon.

Mae and Jimmy Mac had to move like catfish down the Hooch, taking money and handing over cupcakes, baggies of cookies and brownies, and spoonfuls of icing.

Finally there was a lull in the action, and Mae asked, "What happened?"

Davis straightened a row of cookies, the few that were left. "We're about sold out. That's what happened."

"You know what I mean." Mae put her hands on her hips. "Short a couple of hours of community service?"

Jimmy Mac's eyes widened.

"About that," Davis said. He took Mae by the elbow and walked her away from the table so that the others couldn't hear. "It was a stupid thing to say," Davis said.

"Sure was," Mae said, not giving an inch of forgiveness.

"At first it was just hours I had to put in—what the judge ordered." Davis took his hat off and ran his fingers through his hair. Mae could tell that whatever he wanted to say was having a hard time coming out. But why had he been so rude at the grocery store that day and then awful to her in the street? Maybe he pushed people back so that they couldn't see his feelings up close. Sort of like she did.

"But I thought about it," he said. "Miss Fannie, this town—" he hesitated. "And you—you're more than community service."

"You mean you ditched your tryout to come here?" Mae yelled.

"Dial it down a notch, Moore," Davis said. "I don't need everybody knowing my business."

"You gave up your second chance to help Miss Fannie sell cookies?" She whispered this time.

"I left a message with the scout that I wasn't available today," he said. "So yeah, I guess I pretty much did."

Mae hugged him tight, and Davis patted her back. "All right, all right," he said. "Don't cause a scene. It won't help Miss Fannie get her bakery." Davis explained how his former high school coach had planned to meet him at the field before the tryout. Davis had called him and asked for a different favor. The two of them rode through the trailer park, telling everybody about the bake sale and loading up the bus.

"Hey!" Jimmy Mac hollered. "They're comin' back!" He pointed to Jace and Cam.

Davis and Mae ran behind the table while the remaining crowd for both sides gathered around as Jace stepped forward.

He reminded everybody about the prize: The Donut Hole, completely transformed into a bakery and given, free and clear, to the winner.

"It's been a busy last hour," Cam said. "I'm exhausted, and I didn't bake or sell a thing." People laughed. Mae's heart beat fast. "Let's give both teams a round of applause," Jace said, motioning for Savanna and her mother to stand on one side of him and Fannie and Bubba, on the other.

The crowd clapped, and Mae's heart pounded. She looked at Miss Fannie and Bubba. They were holding hands.

Then she looked at the Weatheralls. She could tell Savanna wanted this for her mama as much as Mae wanted it for Miss Fannie.

"We've enjoyed our time in Jessup," Cam said. Jace nodded. "All right, y'all ready to find out the winner?" Cam asked. The crowd hooped and hollered.

This is it, Mae thought. She grabbed Jimmy Mac's and Davis's wrists.

Cam looked at the totals. "Fannie and her team made a total of two hundred and thirty-seven dollars and fifty cents."

Everybody clapped. "We more than doubled sales in the last hour," Jimmy Mac said. Mae nodded. *Was it enough?* she wondered. She squeezed their wrists tighter.

"And Alice Weatherall and her team—" Cam looked at the crowd, then at the paper "—made two hundred and—"

Mae swallowed hard and closed her eyes.

"—five dollars," Cam said. "Fannie Higgins wins!" he shouted.

Bubba put his hand up to high-five Miss Fannie, but she just looked at him and left him hanging. Then she grabbed him around his middle and squeezed hard. Mae, Jimmy Mac, and Davis ran to them and joined in a group hug.

After Fannie's neighbors and the *Flip This Flop* crew congratulated the team, Savanna walked over to Mae. She held out her hand, and Mae shook it. "Congratulations, Mae," she said.

Jimmy Mac smiled at Mae. She knew what he was thinking—maybe they could be friends. Maybe he was right.

The Gilbert brothers said their crew would be back the following week to begin renovations. Miss Fannie was told to decide on décor—color for the walls, type of tables, wall hangings, and other stuff. Miss Fannie looked like she needed to sit down, but Jimmy Mac rescued her, suggesting his mama could help with all that.

Davis and Coach Bailey loaded up the bus to take folks back to Happy Acres, including Beecher and Bubba, who sat in the front row. Davis offered to drop Jimmy Mac and Mae at their houses—make it a one-bus celebration parade, Davis said—but Mae told him she'd wait at the Piggly Wiggly for her mama's shift to end.

Miss Fannie was the last to move toward the bus. She showed Mae a basket with a single baggie of cookies.

"That's all that's left?" Mae asked, taking it. "I'll make sure they don't go to waste," she said, grinning.

Miss Fannie hugged Mae, "We did it, didn't we, girl?"

"It was your baking," Mae said.

"I couldn't have done it without you, Mae Ellen." She let go of Mae and said, "Winning the bakery is wonderful, but I'm most grateful for the hope you gave me."

Mae felt a lump in her throat. "Just let me be your first customer when you open the bakery."

"I promise," Miss Fannie said, stepping on the bus.

As the bus passed, Jimmy Mac waved out the window. "See you at the Hooch tomorrow?" he yelled.

Bubba stuck his head out his window. "What time?" he asked.

Mae laughed. "You name it," she hollered back.

Beecher shoved his head out and yelled, "I'm sleeping 'til noon! How 'bout noon 'o five?"

Mae looked at Jimmy Mac, and they both laughed. "See you there," she said.

CHAPTER TWENTY-FOUR

Mae walked toward the grocery store. *This has been some kind of summer,* she thought. She remembered how it started—seeing Jimmy Mac at the drive-thru prayer. She giggled in her head, remembering how Bubba had almost knocked over the preacher during his visit there.

Jimmy Mac had prayed for his mama, and Davis had prayed for a second chance. *What had Bubba prayed for?* she wondered.

The old Mae would have said something smart-alecky like, "A brain" or "A lifetime supply of Triple Cs." But she was different now. Mae smiled to herself. She hoped he had prayed for some friends because this summer he'd gotten some.

Hope. Such a simple word to explain a world of possibilities. No matter her seemingly unanswered prayers, failed attempts, and crushing disappointments, Mae knew she had to have it. "Faith, hope, and love" is what Preacher Floyd had said. Mae was beginning to see the need for all three.

A fancy car passed her and coasted to the intersection. The light turned red, and the car stopped. Mae didn't recognize the driver or the car. She looked at the license plate. She recognized that. "Atlanta," she mumbled to herself, shaking her head. She looked at the plate again. It had a red frame with the words *Braves* at the bottom.

Mae drew even with the car, waiting for the light to change so that she could cross the street. The driver put down his window. "Excuse me," he said. "Can you point me to the interstate?"

She took a step back from the car. "I'm not supposed to talk to folks from out of town." Mae noticed a red A on the man's shirt pocket.

"That's a good rule to have." He held up his phone. "My phone's dead. Know where I can find an adult to ask?"

"My mama works at the Piggly Wiggly," Mae said, pointing up the street. "She can give you directions."

"Outstanding," he said. "I'll pull in, and you can introduce me to your mother."

Mae watched the man park at the grocery store. He got out and stood by his car, waiting for Mae to catch up. *I wonder,* she thought. *No, it can't be.* But this had been the summer of miracles. Anything could happen—including a stranger looking for a way out of town winding up being the one to finally give Davis his second chance.

"I appreciate the help," he said. "I've been sitting at the high school." He took a folded handkerchief out of his back pocket and wiped the sweat from his face. "After an hour I figured I'd been stood up."

It had to be, Mae said to herself. "I bet you're thirsty," she said as they walked toward the store.

"And hungry," he said.

Mae showed him the cookies. "These might help," she said, holding out the baggie.

"Cookies?" he said. "Those could definitely improve my day."

Mae handed him a Triple C, and he finished it in two bites. The man reached for the other, and Mae pulled the baggie back. "The second one's gonna cost you," she said, grinning. "You interested in making a trade?"

ONE YEAR LATER

The man was indeed a Braves scout sent to take a look at Davis Hampton. He'd gotten his chance to see Davis pitch— followed by a second chocolate-chocolate chip cookie.

He sent Davis back to the Braves and a box of Miss Fannie's Triple Cs to the Braves' home office, where the cookies hit a homerun. He even arranged for Miss Fannie to make her Triple Cs for the team on the Braves' Opening Day.

Miss Fannie and Jimmy Mac's mama led the way to the VIP seats right behind home plate. They were among the other 40,000 Braves' fans—Mae and her family, Jimmy Mac, Bubba, and Beecher. They were all dressed in their yellow T-shirts with "Miss Fannie Favorites and Twila's Treats" printed on the back.

Mae pushed Shelby's wheelchair next to her seat.

"Now pitching for the Atlanta Braves, Davis Hampton," the voice roared over the loudspeaker. Davis's biggest fans stood and cheered.

Beecher sang, "Da da da da da da," And Bubba answered, "Charge!"

Jimmy Mac grinned big at Mae as she shook her head. "We can't take them anywhere," she said.

As Davis walked to the mound, Mae couldn't help but think about last summer and how a bunch of good things came from a few bad things and how drive-thru prayers were answered in ways no one would have ever expected. She turned her head to the sky. "Thank You," she whispered.

Davis looked in the direction of his fans from Jessup and winked.

Mae bent close to her sister. "Watch, Shelby. Davis is about to throw his first strike." Shelby made a humming sound, and Mae's heart leaped when she looked at her sister and saw what might have been a tiny wink back to Davis.

The End

MISS FANNIE'S CHOCOLATE-CHOCOLATE CHIP (TRIPLE C) COOKIES

Ingredients

¾ cup butter (one and a half sticks), softened

¾ cup brown sugar

¼ cup granulated sugar

1 teaspoon vanilla extract

2 large eggs

2¼ cups all-purpose flour

1 small package devil's food (or chocolate) pudding mix, dry

1 teaspoon baking soda

¼ teaspoon salt

2 cups semi-sweet chocolate chips

Directions

Preheat the oven to 350°F.

Using a mixer, cream together the butter and sugars until light and fluffy. Be sure to scrape down the sides of the bowl. Add the vanilla, then add the eggs, one at a time, beating well after each addition.

In a medium bowl, sift together the flour, pudding mix, baking soda, and salt.

Add the flour mixture to the sugar mixture, beating just to combine. Stir in the chocolate chips.

Drop the dough by large rounded spoonfuls onto ungreased baking sheets, spacing the drops at least 2 inches apart.

Bake the cookies for 9 to 12 minutes. They will be done around the edges but gooey in the middle. Cool the cookies and enjoy!

ACKNOWLEDGMENTS

A huge, heartfelt thank you to all who shared in this journey:

My early readers, critique partners, and fabulous writing friends—Alison DeCamp, Elizabeth Dunn, Bronwyn Clark, Dee Romito, Shelly Steig, and Dan Lollis (we will finish the cousin pizza story!). Thank you, marvelous MGBetareaders, especially Becky Appleby, Ronni Arno Blaisdell, Jo Marie Bankston, Rhonda Battenfelder, Jeff Chen, Karen Hallam, Laurie Litwin, Brian Sargent, and Miriam Spitzer for your helpful notes and relentless encouragement for this book and my other stories.

Stacey Graham, the kindest, smartest, and funniest literary agent on the planet! Thank you for trusting me, answering my billion emails (always so quickly), and being gentle with your feedback.

The wonderful Anna Sargeant, editor at B&H Kids. Thank you, Anna, for believing Mae had a story to tell and being so fantastic and comfortable to work with. Thank you to the entire team at B&H, including Michelle Freeman and Diana Lawrence. Many thanks to the talented Alexandra Bye for your cover artwork and to Erin Feldman for your superb copyediting skills.

Keith Benton for your technical support. Thank you for reading and giving me tips on how paramedics respond to emergencies. I could never give your and Kaley's profession the honor it deserves, and any errors are solely mine. And thanks to beautiful Abbie Spurlock, for testing words and phrases on the children you care for as a nanny. Thank you, Parker children!

All the Grayson Elementary and Gwinnet Online Campus students I've worked with throughout the many years. You've kept me grounded in what it's like to be a kid today. And thank you to the teachers at these schools who show me how very important it is to connect with children.

My wonderful friends Peggy Dendy who prayed *Drive-Thru Miracle* all the way to publication and Gail Thayer, the BEST cheerleader ever! Thank you, Gray family, for showing true grace and dedication in how you love sweet Madison. You're an inspiration!

My parents, Sue and Allan Smith, for believing I could write a book that others would want to read. And Sherelene and Tray Scates for letting Buddy come over and play with Lucy so that I could finish those last revisions.

My husband, Chris, and children, Kaley and Jake, for being so patient with my inattention and for never suggesting I give up my dream of writing a book, even though it took a really long time and looked like it might never happen.
And lastly, but most importantly, thanks be to God, the Creator of all things, who gave me a passion to think up stories and provided the faith, hope, and love to see them through.

BOOK CLUB QUESTIONS

1. Reread this excerpt from the end of chapter 2:

> "Shelby okay?" he pressed.
> The ball hit the rim and bounced off. She'd missed a granny shot. "I'll see you around," Mae said, picking up her baseball gear.
> "Hang on," he called after her. "We don't have to talk about it." Jimmy Mac had forgotten the first rule of being Mae's friend: don't ask about her sister.

Why do you think this is a rule in order to be Mae's friend?

2. Even though Shelby can't speak, she shows her personality. How would you describe Shelby to someone who hasn't read *Drive-Thru Miracle*?

3. Mae loved to sit on the large rock at the river when things got scary for Shelby. Do you have a place you like to go to "escape"?

4. Mae says, "I get scared sometimes." Davis responds by saying, "Everybody does. Fear seems to show up most when we put faith in the wrong things" (chapter 12). What do you think Davis means by this?

5. More than one character has a secret in this story. What are these secrets, and why do you think the characters keep them from others?

6. Mae thinks about her ninth birthday wish every day. The memory pops up; she pushes it down. Up. Down (chapters 3 and 15). What wish did Mae make on her ninth birthday? How does she feel about the wish?

7. What does Mae want her sister to know more than anything (chapter 3)? Why is it so important to Mae?

8. Mae's family seems positive and even joyful despite their many challenges. Why do you think this is?

9. Do you think hope can change someone's situation? Has hope ever changed something for you?

10. Some of the characters in the story change their assumptions about other characters. (Example: Mae's daddy changed what he thought of Mae's ability to take care of Shelby.) Can you think of any more examples?

11. Fannie shows love for many characters in the story. For example, she agrees to make the anniversary cake for Mae's parents for free even when she is facing financial difficulties. Why do you think she does this? Can you think of any more examples?

12. Why does Mae's daddy refer to the contest between Fannie and Mrs. Weatherall as a David and Goliath match-up (chapter 19)?

13. Davis decides to help Fannie win the bake sale (chapter 23) even if it might cost him a second chance at a baseball career. Why do you think he changes his mind? Do you think the choice was hard for him?

14. If you could pick any character in the story to be your friend, who would you choose? Why?

15. In what ways does Mae change throughout *Drive-Thru Miracle*? What do you think is the cause of these changes?

16. Initially, Bubba doesn't want anyone to know that he likes to bake. Why is that? Why does he finally agree to let others know? Is there something you like to do, but you think others might make fun of you if they knew about it?

17. Fannie and Bubba have a shared love of baking. Do you like to bake? What is your favorite thing to bake or eat that is baked by someone else?

18. Preacher Floyd's son died in a horrible accident. How would you answer the question, "Why do bad things happen to good people?"

19. There are times in the story when it seems that Mae has lost her faith. For example, in chapter 1 Mae talks about her sister: *Mae decided then that praying didn't work and there*

wasn't any use in hoping things could be different. And in chapter 9, when Mae sees the Donut Hole has been sold, she says, *"Stupid prayer! All it does is get your hopes up," she said. "Nothing's ever gonna change."* Why do you think she's lost faith in prayer? Does that change by the end of the story? Have you ever struggled with your faith?

20. What is the miracle (or miracles) in *Drive-Thru Miracle*? Have you ever witnessed or asked for a miracle? What happened?